Thirteen Paths
A Halloween Anthology

Jess Boldt

Andy Lockwood

Jenifer Lynn

Published by Last Leaf Books, 2023

Other books by Jess Boldt:

Disonia

Other books by Andy Lockwood:

Empty Hallways

House of Thirteen, Book One

At Calendar's End: Omnibus

Threshold

Other books by Jenifer Lynn:

Winter's Resonance: A Series of Echoes, Book I

TABLE OF CONTENTS

Timber & Stone

Andy Lockwood

"Where are we going?" The pirate white-knuckled the hilt of his sword as a skeleton dragged him along.

"You'll find out when we get there!"

The pirate groaned; the skeleton laughed and pulled harder, eliciting a yelp from the witch at the end of the chain.

"Is it going to be scary?" The witch trailed behind, her purple hair bouncing in the breeze as the pirate clung to her broom.

"It's Halloween! Of course it is!" Shea laughed louder, the skeleton face paint giving the appearance of a jaw unhinged, ducking between trick-or-treaters as he diverted into a cul-de-sac. The conjoined trio skirted crowds of children begging for candy and moved to the overgrown driveway at the end of the lane.

The gate was held fast by heavy chain – only partly to keep trespassers away. Mostly, it was to keep the gate from falling off the fence. The path to the house was hardly visible, choked with weeds as it blended into the overgrown yard. The house beyond was hardly a house any longer. The brickwork remained; its exposed edges softened by time. Four exterior walls and two chimneys remained, marking the place where a home once stood. The French doors had long ago fallen from their hinges; the windows smashed out by vandals decades ago. Framing jutted sporadically from the wall, partially outlining the staircase's ascension – before it and the second-story landing collapsed into the basement. It was hard to imagine the parts that remained as a turn-of-the-century hallmark of construction, but such was the story of most ruins.

"There it is," Shea spoke with a quiet reverence as he approached the gate. He let his friends fall behind. He knew they would come closer when they were ready.

"There *what* is?" Titus asked, raising his eye patch to observe the mess of rotted wood and weathered brick. He shared a look with Willow, who shrugged under her oversized hat.

"They say the ghosts are still in there," Shea broke the relative silence, fiddling with his skeleton gloves as the three of them stared up at the derelict property. Behind them, children laughed and squealed all around the neighborhood. They charged up sidewalks and raided houses until every house had been ransacked.

All but one.

Whether subconsciously or not, travelers took a wide berth around the abandoned lot, all but consciously avoiding eye contact with the hollow structure. For all anyone knew, its only inhabitants for the last couple decades were birds, bats, and the occasional rodent.

It was uncomfortable how the sounds of trick-or-treaters could be all around them and so distant at the same time. It left Shea unsettled and surprisingly alone, despite bringing his friends here to experience this exact feeling.

"They say, if the ghosts join you for trick-or-treating, you'll join them shortly after."

"Why would you say that?" Willow shuddered, smacking Shea with her pointed hat, but never taking her eyes off the brickwork.

"Relax; nobody says that." Titus scoffed, slicing at weeds with his plastic sword.

"Sure they do."

"Okay, who?"

"People."

"People like who?"

Finally, Shea broke his fixed gaze to look at Titus, giving the other boy the satisfaction of a job well done.

"I don't know who, okay? I just heard."

"Oh sure. That doesn't sound made up at all."

"Would you two stop?" Willow gave Shea a shove, knocking him off balance and into Titus, who shoved back. Willow squealed and teetered – then shrieked.

Both boys turned to see her wheeling back away from a

ghost they hadn't noticed before. It was sitting on a low rock wall, its head hung forward. It did not look like a happy ghost.

"Um, hello." Willow's voice was timid, quaking as much as her hands as she attempted a wave.

The ghost looked up, practically amorphous except for the two large, dark eye holes. They looked painted on – as if the sheet had no holes, but two black ovals painted onto the fabric.

"Happy Halloween!" Shea betrayed any nervousness with the confidence in his voice. "Why are you sitting here by yourself?"

The ghost regarded them for a long moment before it shrugged, the ruffle of shoulders making the rest of the large white sheet billow before settling again. It seemed to melt a little, head sloping forward once more.

"Are you lost?" Titus asked gently. Shea wondered where the question came from, slowly picking up on the smallest sway in the ghost's white folds as if feet were swinging somewhere underneath the long sheet.

The ghost paused long enough to shake its head.

The group said nothing as they looked from one to the other, exchanging glances. It was a silent discussion, the kind only the closest friends can have. Even through the muddle of grease paint and accessories, they all knew they should be going.

The silence continued until Willow cleared her throat.

"We should probably –"

"He's right." The ghost didn't look up, but it did stop swinging its feet. It remained stock still while they questioned its words.

Willow turned to look at her friends before returning to the ghost.

"Him?" She pointed at Shea. Titus looked at Shea and rolled his eyes.

"Him." The ghost raised its head, nodding slowly. In the daylight, the eyes might have been comically oversized, but in the waning light of an autumn evening, they looked hollow, hungry.

Before anyone had the courage to inquire further, its gaze turned toward the house. Their collective gaze followed, all staring up the path at the bones of the old structure.

"They're still in there."

Shea shuddered, a sudden cold creeping into his heart. He wanted to ask if they felt it too but didn't dare. The sun was gone, the sky was darkening, and there was a ghost – real or fabricated – telling them about the house. All he could do was join his friends in staring helplessly at the property. He waited for the moment to pass, for the cold to release its grip on his heart, but the moment only seemed to draw itself out longer.

"It's never like they say. No one alive knows the real story."

There was a small, inconspicuous jab, as Titus elbowed his friend in the ribs.

"Told you so," Titus sneered and said nothing more.

Willow swallowed, her mouth dry. "Do you know the real story?"

The ghost turned back, cocking its head slightly as it regarded her. It nodded. A cold shiver raced down her body and she shuddered. The shiver seemed to flow through Titus and into Shea.

"Would you tell us?"

Both boys looked at Willow, but the wide brim of her hat blocked their hard stares. For a long moment, no one moved. Shea didn't realize he was holding his breath until he gasped for air. They watched as the ghost shifted, pointing a sheet-draped arm at Shea.

"Him first."

Shea stumbled; it was like being knocked over by some unseen force. He had no idea if it was real, or just the shock of being called out. Willow and Titus each grabbed an arm to keep him from toppling over in a heap of costume bones.

"Here's your chance," Titus laughed, but the sound was as empty and hollow as the holes in the sheet that watched them now.

"I'd rather not."

"Go on," Titus sounded more insistent than taunting. He almost sounded afraid.

Shea swallowed hard. "No one knows the real story. It happened ages ago."

"You better make up a good one then." Willow tugged his arm and twisted around him, pushing him to the front of the group, where he had the ghost's full attention.

Shea wiped his skeleton gloves on his thighs, the sweat collecting in the fabric, offering him no comfort. He reached up to wipe the sweat from his brow and paused. His face was a mural of black and white grease paint, wiping at it would only smear it everywhere and provide less comfort than sweaty skeleton palms. He shook his hands out at his sides and took a deep breath.

"Okay," Cold fell over him as he exhaled. "So, the house is old, right? Over a hundred. But it wasn't always. Back when the house was new – at least by comparison – it went up for sale."

"Why would anyone sell this house?" Willow looked up at the remains of the structure.

"They didn't. The city did, eventually."

"Why?" Willow looked back at Shea.

"The house sat vacant for months. The previous owners left without a trace." Shea ignored her, continuing on. "The car was still in the driveway; food still in the fridge."

"They vanished?" Titus questioned; incredulity now gone from his tone.

"They vanished."

Shea wanted to enjoy this; he wished he could. He had been dreaming about a moment like this the whole month, but from the corner of his eye, he could see the ghost start to creep closer, its attention rapt. Shea had to suppress a shudder and remember there was a story to tell.

"Eventually, a new family moved in. They made the house their own." He paused, seeing the ghost had drifted closer still. "That's when the strange things started going on."

Almost hypnotically, the pirate, witch, and ghost found themselves standing in formation as they listened to Shea tell his story.

"It started small; a chair out of place, a crooked frame. But slowly, they realized that something otherworldly was going on."

Willow listened, hands wringing nervously. Titus' arms were folded across his chest, but the occasional shiver betrayed his defensive stance. The ghost continued to stare, billowing as Shea tried to ignore it.

"It suddenly made sense why the house sold so cheap; why it was so easy to get it. Now, the family was stuck. They didn't have money to buy a new house; they couldn't go anywhere else. They were trapped in a house full of ghosts."

Titus and Willow shuddered together. The ghost stared.

"The spirits continued to haunt the family, growing bolder in their deeds, until one day, a fire broke out. The mom had been working late, the dad had just stepped out for a minute. Their son was by himself when the ghosts trapped him. He was still trapped inside when the fire engulfed the house."

Willow's throat was dry; her voice hushed. "He died?"

Shea nodded.

Titus leaned into Willow. She leaned back against him. Their shoulders seemed to loosen, the tension ebbing out with the conclusion of the story.

"No."

All three of them jumped, the ghost between them somehow momentarily forgotten.

"No?" Shea swallowed. He knew it was a fabrication, but now, he wasn't sure if he wanted the truth if it came from those hollow eyes.

The ghost seemed to float as it closed the distance between itself and Shea. A breeze rose around the group, pushing leaves and dust, but the hem of the dirty sheet remained still.

"No one disappeared. There were no ghosts in the house before the fire."

Willow and Titus could only stare as the scene

unfolded before them. Shea gulped; eyes wide. He wanted to retreat, but he could only fall back as far as the rusty gate.

"Do you know what happened?" Willow asked, a quaver in her voice.

The white sheet turned to her, fixing her with its empty gaze.

"The little boy died; that's true. His parents got the house from his grandparents. They died in the house; one from old age, the other from loneliness. His mom grew up in the house. She loved the idea of coming back home and raising her boy there. His dad hated it. He called it a handout."

Slowly, Shea navigated the path around the billowing sheet until the friends were pressed together again.

"His mom worked and his dad drank. His dad resented her for her job and her parents and her house. He didn't hate the boy but sometimes he forgot what he was angry about, and the boy was just there."

The ghost seemed to shrink into itself even as an edge crept into its voice. It seemed small and fragile, but all the same; sharp and mean. The other three hovered as close as they dared.

"Every Halloween, his mom would sew a new costume for him, all by herself. It was his favorite time of year, better than Christmas. The last year, he was a cowboy. He wore the costume all day, twirling his silver six-shooter guns for the whole school. He was so busy making a show of his guns, he didn't realize until he got home that he forgot his hat. He wanted to go back to school and get it, but his mom was at work and his dad was passed out. Still, he wanted his hat for trick-or-treating."

Shea couldn't stop staring into the ghost's eyes. As the darkness crept in, they seemed to grow bigger, deeper. He wasn't sure anyone was behind them.

"His dad was so angry. Angry about being woke up, and being needed, and so many other things the boy didn't understand. His father locked him in the closet under the stairs to punish him. The boy was so sad; he cried hard and loud. That only made his dad angrier."

They looked at each other, sharing another silent conversation. None of them liked where this story was going.

"Stop, please," Willow whispered, reaching out to clasp hands with the boys. "I don't think I want to hear anymore."

"He begged and pleaded. He only wanted to go trick-or-treating."

The three children clasped hands, squeezing tight. The tension – and the sudden fury of the wind around them – seemed to increase as the ghost's voice grew darker, harder.

"His dad threw his drink at the closet door. It splashed everywhere; the glass hit a lamp and broke the bulb." The ghost paused and the wind died with its words for a moment. It turned to look at the remains of the house and did not turn back to the other children.

Shea winced; Willow was crushing his fingers. Her bottom lip quivered as she stared at the apparition. He turned to Titus, who was equally agog. They were rapt, waiting for the next word to be spoken, afraid of the rest of the story.

For his part, Shea was practically frozen with fear. The implications that were rising in front of him were more dreadful than anything he could have dreamed up himself.

"It was such a big fire."

The wind died with the ghost's words. Willow broke down into sobs, kneeling on the concrete walkway. Titus happened a glance at Shea. The look said that they should go – now. But Shea wasn't done. There was one more question left to ask; one last bit of the story he would tell for the future.

The ghost continued to stare up at the derelict site, practically motionless in the now-still evening. Shea took a tentative step forward. When the ghost didn't react, he took another step.

One baby step after another closed the distance between them, Shea's fingers stretching forward, eyes greedily focused on the white sheet.

He heard sounds behind him. Titus and Willow were

trying to get his attention. He would not be deterred; would not be distracted. It felt like a year had passed before his fingers finally came within grasping distance. He could feel the cool air on his sweaty hands. All the moisture in his body must have been wicking to his gloves because his throat was dry, his eyes stinging.

"Don't!" He barely heard Willow's whispered plea. Normally, he'd give in when she was serious, but he couldn't. Not tonight. This was the opportunity of a lifetime.

Before anyone could say anything else, he snapped his wrist and grabbed hold of the sheet. He tugged, throwing his arm upward, and snapping down again, to give the sheet a proper arc.

It felt like cool mist between his fingers, like how airplanes must feel cutting through the clouds. The sheet followed the path Shea designated, the fabric pulling at the form underneath it, creating a silhouette within. The face turned, its shape disappearing from the wisping fabric. Shea felt his breath catch in his throat but dared not close his eyes. The fabric billowed, rising off the figure beneath to reveal – nothing.

Perhaps it was hope, fleeting desperation, or a trick of the waning light, but Shea swore for a single moment that he saw a pair of woeful eyes staring into his before they vanished into the darkness. The ghostly sheet cascaded to the ground, dissolving into a gentle fog before dissipating into the night.

Shea stood watching, his mouth open in shock and wonder. The jab came out of nowhere, the small bony knuckles of an irate witch boxing his kidney.

"Don't ever do that again!" Willow shouted, picking up her broom and whacking him in the thigh. "Not ever again! Do you hear me?"

Shea yelped, dropping to a knee, trying to hold his side and massage out the charley horse in his leg at the same time. Titus took Willow by the shoulders, holding her back from attacking a third time. He was trying to keep his cool for the sake of the group, but Shea could see the wildness in his eyes.

"Can we go home now?" Titus sighed, the breath shuddering its way out of him.

They stepped into a dwindling flow of trick-or-treaters, following the current back toward home, the sound and activity a drastic change to the cold quiet at the end of the lane.

Unseasonable

Jenifer Lynn

"Who would be trick or treating in this?"

Tate looked up from the candle she had just lit. "No one," she said, blowing out the match before the flame reached her fingers. "No one trick or treats at these apartments anyway, let alone during a snowstorm."

The freak blizzard had started in the afternoon, thick flakes falling hard and fast. By sunset they were trapped inside by more than a foot of snow. Heavy and wet, it clung to walls and trees, coating their newly carved jack-o-lanterns and pulling at branches. Tate was certain it was a tree branch that had taken out the power to the apartment complex. She had just pulled the popcorn from the microwave when she'd heard a distant crack and the apartment had gone dark, throwing a wrench in their scary movie Halloween plans.

"And yet..." David stood at the patio door, eyeing the darkness beyond. Tate finished lighting the last candle and joined him, following his gaze.

Her patio sat six feet above the snow covered ground and faced the diminutive "lake" that was the centerpiece of the complex. It stretched about fifty yards across, and was currently giving its best effort to make tiny waves in the blowing snow. Circling the water were twenty two-and-a-half-story buildings housing eight apartments each. Tate watched as candles and flashlights flickered to life in a dozen windows. Dim solar-powered security lamps joined the ambient light from the nearby city, bouncing off the falling snow to bathe the scene in an eerie twilight glow.

"It's crazy out there," she said, feeling the chill permeating the sliding glass door.

"But look," David said, pointing to the building directly across the water.

Four figures, just shadows against the snow, were moving between buildings.

"Jesus," Tate said, a chill moving from her skin to her spine.

"Those kids are going to freeze to death trying to trick or treat out there." They watched as the figures passed by an apartment with darkened windows and moved behind a wall that obscured the door to the upper apartment. "Where are their parents?"

Tate shook her head, watching as a flashlight from the upper apartment made its way across the living room, and out of sight. The light came back briefly, flickering and bouncing against the walls before disappearing again.

"Maybe someone will convince them to go home," Tate said. "Hopefully."

The crackle of shuffling cards startled her, pulling her attention from the window and back to the candlelit table. David shuffled one more time and dealt out five cards to each of them. "We're going to play the spookiest game of Halloween strip poker you've ever seen."

"The hell we are," Tate said, pulling a chair under her. "We're going to lose heat in this apartment fast. If anything, I plan on putting on *more* clothes."

David shot her a mischievous grin. "Then you'll just have to win, won't you?"

The scent of pumpkin and cinnamon filled the room as the Halloween-themed candles sizzled on the center of the table. Tate played her hand halfheartedly, showing no joy in beating him twice in a row.

David watched her, chewing on his cheek. "I know this wasn't how you wanted to spend Halloween. At least we got to carve jack-o-lanterns before the blackout, though, right?"

"Yeah, I suppose." She glanced out onto the patio, barely able to see the pumpkins under layers of new snow.

His eyebrows raised and he reached into his pocket. "Hey, maybe we could watch some spooky movies on my phone!"

Tate shook her head, rolling a cold kernel of popcorn between her fingers. "I doubt it. Service here is pretty spotty."

He shrugged. "It's worth a shot, right?"

Tate stood and looked out the patio door again. Many of the apartments across the lake had gone dark again. The inhabitants likely turned in early in the hopes that power would be restored by morning.

Not likely, she thought. She couldn't see utility vehicles risking the weather for anything beyond the most dire circumstances.

Shadows moving along the north side of the lake, about 5 buildings away, caught her eye. "They're still out there," she whispered. Closer now than they had been across the lake, any details were still lost to the elements.

David joined her at the window. "Must be really warm costumes," he said.

The snow had to be nearly two feet deep by now, but they seemed to glide above it effortlessly. They paused, looking up at one dark apartment, and then moved on to the next, congregating together on the small walk in front of the door.

A candle flickered at the landing window as the occupant came downstairs to answer the door. Tate saw her briefly, pale face lit by candlelight, before a gust of wind cast the scene into shadow.

A scream joined the howling wind, ripping across the lake to reach her ears. Adrenaline shot through Tate, lifting her briefly in the air and leaving her shaking. "What was that?" she asked, panic cracking her voice.

"It's fine," David said. He grabbed his phone from the table and showed her the buffering screen. "It's just my phone. It's trying to play a spooky movie." He put an arm around her, rubbing her shoulder. "Seems like it did its job, right?"

Tate frowned at him, unable to stop her trembling. "I don't think that came from your phone," she said.

"Come on," he said. "There's nothing else it could have been, okay?"

"It sounded like it came from..." she trailed off as she looked out the glass door again. The door to the apartment was open and vacant. The candle she had been holding rolled across the walk, taken by the wind. "Where did they go?"

"Holy shit," David said, a hint of fear creeping into his voice. "How did he get up there?"

Tate turned her attention to the next building. Three of the shadows were encroaching on the door to apartment C. The fourth was on the elevated patio, its silhouette dark against the lantern-lit sliding door. He looked like a teenager, taller than a child, and gangly with unnaturally long arms. As she watched, he lifted one arm to place a long-fingered hand on the glass.

"There's no way to get up there unless you can jump really high," David was saying. "I know, I've tried."

A moment later, the lantern in the living room of apartment C went out, hiding the figure on the patio.

"They've really dedicated themselves to this Halloween mischief," David was saying, but Tate could hear the layer of doubt underneath the words. "When I was a teen, I wouldn't even TP if it was raining, despite the fact that wet toilet paper is the perfect TP prank. I didn't care. No getting my hair wet, you know?"

Tate turned from the window and watched David. He was pacing from the living room, to the dining room, and back again. The living room was dark, and on his second trip back, he grabbed a candle to take with him and fend off the shadows. He was talking fast, trying to talk his way back from what they both thought they were seeing outside.

"I don't think those are teenagers, David."

He stopped, frozen to the spot and turned a white face to meet her gaze. "Of course they are."

Another scream echoed through the complex. This one, much closer. They both looked at his phone on the table, the wheel turning on the same scene it had been trying to load for ten minutes.

"We have to call the police," he said. "They're out there harassing people. Plus they're probably going to freeze to death."

"No one's coming," Tate murmured, tuning him out and turning back to the window. They were two buildings away now, and she could see them with more clarity. Darkly clothed, wearing masks with huge, distorted grins imprinted into the plastic. The sideways blowing snow didn't seem to phase them, briefly clinging to them before clumping up and falling off as they moved from one apartment to the next. They would stop to look at windows, seeming to discuss with each other before deciding which doors to knock on.

They again skipped an apartment with dark, empty windows, instead choosing one that was lit with a color-changing LED lamp. Tate had subconsciously watched it change from green, to purple, to white, and then orange, since the power went out. Someone bored, or attempting to keep the Halloween spirit alive.

Tate wondered if it was her imagination, hearing the three loud knocks ring out above the whistling wind. The door opened a moment later, her neighbor, a young single man she had had brief conversations with in the laundry room, opened the door and bathed the scene in green light. His expression shifted from curiosity to pure terror, enhanced by the sickly hue.

He opened his mouth to scream and the figures converged on him, snuffing out the light.

"The light," Tate whispered. She turned away from the door, eyes wide, and began blowing out the candles. "It's the light, David. They're going to apartments that have light."

She blew out the candles on the table, then the one in the bathroom before trying to take the candle away from David. He flinched.

"But it'll be dark!" he said, his voice high and plaintive.

Another series of knocks, only one building over now. "That's the point," Tate hissed, trying to pull the candle out of his hands. He fought against her and it fell to the carpet, hot wax spilling into the fibers, the flame extinguishing. A dim light on the table caught her eye, and she grabbed his phone, struggling to turn it off as another scream, just across the garden, drowned out the wind.

She wanted to close the blinds, but she was afraid to draw attention to them. Instead, she backed away from the windows, pulling David with her to sit against the opposite wall. He whimpered and shrank down against the wall with her, trying to be invisible in the dark. She squeezed her eyes shut, tears falling down her cheeks, and waited.

They were coming. She could hear them in the other apartments in her building. Hear them moving around outside, not footsteps, but movement through the snow, through the storm.

The creak of wood on her patio.

"No, no no no," David was whimpering.

Tapping on the glass.

The door downstairs shook as three loud knocks reverberated against it.

It's got to be a prank. Tate thought to herself, hearing the tap of fingers against glass again. *Just a prank, open your eyes and show them you aren't scared.*

Tate opened her eyes.

It wasn't a prank. It wasn't a mask.

The creature's too-big grin grew larger as it locked eyes with her, lit orange by the flickering LED candle in her perfectly carved jack-o-lantern.

Next Stop Home

Jess Boldt

The glass window of the old train depot radiated orange with the late October sunset. The red bricks of the small building slowly faded into deeper shades of blue as the town's streetlights reported for their nightly watch detail. Beneath the hill at which the depot sat, the sounds of children racing home with bags, pillowcases, and buckets of candy rose to a triumphant crescendo, then faded as porch lights went dark and Jack-O-Lanterns flickered and faded.

Billy, a boy of twelve years, watched this annual dance of light and shadow from his position on the iron train tracks below his feet. He adjusted his brown wool cap and pulled the matching jacket tighter around his adolescent body. He stared at his leather brown shoes as one foot hesitantly took its first step off the rail and onto the stony gravel below. The right shoe followed and surpassed the first, and as if not to be undone, the left shoe responded in turn. Soon the uneven gravel gave way to the crunch of autumn leaves over browning grass.

Billy pushed his hands into the pockets of his jacket and walked past the depot. Its small overhead light was pushing away the night with a soft white glow, while attracting the last moths of the year. Billy stopped and turned back to the tracks and tried to find more depth in the pockets. With forced conviction, he turned back around and walked down the hill which led into town.

In minutes, he was in downtown Thornsville, a small district by any measure, populated by two-story brick buildings which were illuminated by street lights set at equal frequency from each other. At the end of the street was a roundabout that would shoot off traffic into different areas of the town during the day. Tonight was void of traffic and sound except for the electric hum of the street lights and the sound of a boy's footsteps. As Billy made his way down the sidewalk, he passed Drumple's Hardware, a proud building that seemed just a bit more lively than the rest. He stopped and looked into the window, not at the hand saws, hammers, or rakes that were on crowded display, but the paper decorations taped to the large pane window. A scarecrow with a pumpkin head, frozen in a sun-bleached smile. Next to that stood a skeleton posed as if he was trapped in a rubbery dance that defied any anatomical reality, yet would make sense to any child walking by. A slight smile bent itself towards his cheek as he continued forward.

Before long he stood at the roundabout. He was close enough to see the wilted flower bed and stone war memorial plaque that stood in the center of it, but his eyes were focused on the second outlet. Walking along the cement edges, passing the first exit, and shooting himself off the second. Commerce quickly gave way to houses with wooden porches and darkened, hollowed pumpkins. After a few turns down tree lined streets, past more than a few wooden fences, he came upon a small two-story house, bathed in the blue light of the moon just enough to reveal the chipped white paint that covered every surface except for the wooden porch. There were no pumpkins, no decorations, no interior lights. The house just stood silently and Billy stood just as silent, staring at the structure.

"That's your house, young man?" a gravelly voice inquired, sparking Billy to jolt and grasp his chest. The alarmed boy turned quick around to see an older man, his face marked with the evidence of emotion and time. He wore what looked to be a suit, the color and pattern undeterminable in the moonlight.

"Yes, I mean, well, it..." Billy stopped and took a moment to calm his nerves. "I'm not trespassing, if that's what you mean."

"Nobody's accusing you of trespassing. I was just curious. Besides, curfew ends at dawn," the old man said as if he was trying to contain a slight laugh. "We're nighthawks, you and I. I always liked this place much more when the sun sets," the old man said, his smile widening.

Billy looked up at the old man, his eyes adjusting to the darkness. He could see now that the man wore a grey suit with a striped pattern of white thread. His hair was white but not thin as most men his age. He straightened out, revealing himself to be taller than Billy had originally thought, perhaps around six-foot-five or even a hair taller.

"I didn't mean to give a start, just out for a little walk. A man can get a lot of thinking done, just walking around these streets. Or sometimes it helps a man not to think, which can be equally as enjoyable, sometimes more," the man said while holding out his hand. "Forgive me, my name is Albert Sands. And your name, young sir?"

Billy slowly reached out and grasped the older man's hand. "Bill, um, William Shepard, sir," he responded.

"Pleasure to meet you, Billy," Albert said as he released his grip, then turned his attention to the house. "It's a fine place, that house. It has character and I'm betting a lot of history. So, is that your place?"

Billy's face grew darker as his features dropped. "I left some time ago."

"Don't tell me a young man like yourself ran away. Perhaps to join up with the circus? Or set off to the sea to explore foreign lands," Albert playfully inquired.

"Nothing like that. I just couldn't stay there any longer. But I'm back now, this is where I belong," Billy replied.

Albert Sands studied the house for a moment, tracing the outline of the house with his finger. He then looked down at Billy. "I see what you mean, like I said, a lot of character. You know something, most places are built with character in mind, but the design isn't actually what creates the actual character. You know what does? No? It's time. The passage of time and those who witnessed it."

Billy looked at him and shrugged. "I guess. Well, I should be getting inside. I'll see you around," he said as he started towards the house. As he moved forward, he felt a weight to his steps. Each step becoming heavier until he found it difficult to move an inch. Sighing, he turned around to face Albert Sands. "I guess I'm not quite ready yet."

Albert smiled at him warmly. "I guess not. Well, there's still time before curfew. Tell you what, perhaps you can walk back downtown with me. I'm old and subject to time's cruel hand. I could trip on a curve and bust my teeth out. Who knows. Maybe by then, you would have worked up the courage to go home."

Billy stared blankly at the man, his lips began to protest but before a sound of air could leave his mouth, he noticed his feet starting to move towards the man, the heaviness of his steps dissipating into the cool October night.

The two walked at a slow rhythm towards downtown. Albert pointed out a large blue Victorian house on the corner. Billy kept pace, his light feet wanting to race past the man, but he found himself keeping pace with each slow step. "See that house, my young guide? That's where Patricia Melkin lived for many years. Her father was a cruel man, and she grew to be an equally cruel woman. That's often the case, awful things passed down from one generation to another. Ah, but sometimes nature has a way of surprising you. You see, she had a daughter of her own, Helen, and despite her cruel mother and equally cruel father, she grew up to be the kindest woman this town ever saw. You see, her father struck her mother down with a meat cleaver then took his own life. She inherited everything at the tender age of fifteen. She spent her time and fortune helping the poor and in need here. She built a park just so everyone could enjoy Sundays in the warm months," Albert explained, then shook his head. "Real tragedy when the TB took her at thirty and some years. The entire town came out for her funeral. It was quite the moving sight."

Billy stared at the house as it slowly went by. After some time, they found themselves at the roundabout. Albert gestured towards the war memorial plaque in the center. "Young Vincent Shoemaker, a real firecracker, that one. First light of dawn he would be out running errands for Mr. Dumple. He was always saving money for a girl, er, perhaps several girls. He would buy charms, licorice, well, you name it. And with those little trinkets he would capture hearts.

Well, then there was the war. Vincent set off towards Europe. Poor soul never even saw a trench... Well, maybe that was a real blessing, come to think of it. Died in training. A shell went off, never knew what hit him." Albert smiled then softly laughed. "I can tell you one thing, you've never seen so many sobbing young women at a funeral before. Turns out there probably wasn't a single female in town that he didn't woo at some point."

They moved past the exit that led to downtown and towards the next. "Mr. Sands, we're going past downtown," Billy meekly protested while keeping the methodical pace.

"Please, son. Call me Albert, or even Al. Always liked the sound of that. Don't worry, we're just taking a different route," the old man replied. "It won't take long. We'll have you back well before curfew."

The two walked past onto Jensen Road and into other neighborhoods. Albert would sporadically point out a house or business, followed by a macabre anecdote regarding the previous occupants, including one that Billy found particularly grim involving a family of seven being sent to their graves by the Spanish Flu. Billy felt a rock grow in his stomach once he realized where the end of the street led, Tompkins Graveyard. "Sir, um, Al, I do not wish to go this way," he protested, unable to break pace with the man.

"Nobody ever does, Billy. Unfortunately that is the fate for most of us. Do you remember what I said about walking at night and not thinking?"

"Just that it was sometimes better, I think," Billy replied as the panic rose up from that rock in his stomach.

"Indeed. If you've lived as long as I have, there are many things done that are best forgotten, even if just for a little while. Even if you have to do them again. And between you and me, I find Halloween the best time for such walks," he stated absently.

Billy struggled with his thoughts, each one jumping in and out of his head like the rare autumn moths bouncing onto the lamp's surface just to hop off just as quickly. No matter how hard he fought his feet, they would not obey him. They moved up the hill, the iron rod gates of the cemetery in sight. He could make out the white church on the hill, surrounded by creeping and violent trees that had shed their leaves, each branch threatening to stretch and devour the building. It stood with its large vertical windows on its side. He could make out the door, above it, just below the steeple, a sign. Although it was too dark to read, he had seen it on more Sundays than he could remember. If there was more light, it would have read, 'Thornsville Church of Christ' on a modest wooden frame. One hundred feet, eighty feet, forty feet. Ten. Then a jumping thought hit his mind, not even a fully birthed thought, a word. 'Halloween.'

"I just want to trick-or-treat again, Albert, I just want to run with my friends, collect candy. I want to dress up as something frightening. It's still Halloween, isn't it?"

Albert shook his head then stopped his stride, and in doing so, Billy's stride stopped as well. Albert's wrinkled lips parted, "Halloween. Yes, it's my favorite holiday as well. You know the Celtics believed that is when the world of flesh and the world of spirit isn't impregnable. I always liked those folks." He shook his head slightly then smiled. "I guess it's every young man's prerogative to stay out past curfew. Tell you what, follow me back downtown and we can skip this portion of our tour for now."

Albert turned around and headed back, away from the garden of carved stone. Billy found himself following again, but his steps felt neither heavy nor light. He kept walking, but was now slightly off pace from the man. He wondered if he was walking because he was meant to or if he just was curious where this new detour would lead him.

When they got back to the center of town, the birds had begun chirping at the blackness of the predawn. Albert sat easily on a wooden bench across from Dumple's Hardware. Billy found himself sitting next to him. The old man pointed his finger at the hardware store and traced the outline of the brick building with it.

"Mr. Dumple, Edward Dumple. He met his end when he fell asleep with a cigar in his mouth. Another late night going over inventory. Well, that cigar hit a pile of rags. The entire building and half the block went up in flames. That one cigar claimed eight souls that night," Albert stated.

"What do you mean? Went up in flames? Dumple's is still there, like it has always been," Billy protested.

"Nothing stands forever, Billy. But, yes, things do stand for a time. And that's what gives things 'character', I suppose. It's the time they stood, no matter how long, against the march of times. Decades, years, days, hours, seconds, all drops of water, weathering us down, giving us character," Albert said with a sincere smile.

At that moment, the first rays of light from the sunrise over a distant hill began to illuminate the town. "Well, it's curfew, young master William, you're about to see a sight few have had the privilege. Have you ever noticed that you can almost see the way things were when you walk through an old neighborhood at night?"

The sunlight washed over the town. Everywhere it touched, the world changed. The first rays hit the top of Dumple's Hardware, or what was now a strange four-story building made of glass and metal. As the light changed the building, Billy could make out a sign that said 'First National Bank of Thornsville.' Petrified by the sight, he dared not move as the light erased a green and tan Buick

Roadster, replacing it with a nearby vehicle of the sorts Billy had never seen or dreamed of. It was painted the brightest red he ever saw. Its lines were curved and slim. If anything, it looked like something out of space comic.

"That's the thing with time, it just keeps going, eventually changing everything. Everything has to move on, and it's my job to make sure it does. That includes you, Billy," Albert stated as Billy lowered his head. "You see, that train hit you nearly eighty-four years ago. And the entire town came out, well most of the people at least. Mrs. Hathworth never really forgave you for jumping into her hedges," he said, letting out a small laugh. "But I guess one rule has already been broken, and it's the prerogative of every young man to break a few rules, I guess it's the same for us old men as well. I tell you what, you can stay at your post, waiting for Halloween, waiting to walk among the shadows of time, and when you're ready, and you very well will be after a while, let me know and I will escort you home. After all, what would this world be without a few haunts, especially on Halloween?"

Billy looked up at the man, tears forming in his eyes. "I, I think I understand. I would love to see one more Halloween night here, maybe two."

"See a hundred if you wish. But now that you know me, there will be a night where the shadows cease to be nostalgic, and you will want to see what is beyond."

"Beyond?" Billy asked. "Is there trick-or-treating in, um, beyond, Albert?"

"I've already broken enough rules for you tonight, but I'll just say that it's not as lonely of a road as some think. In fact, everyone is on it eventually. Now run back to your post, this world isn't for you," Albert said as he rose to his feet.

Billy stood as well, then nodded. He sprinted past the changing world, his feet moving by his own will, he was sure of it now. Each stride brought a new year, a new decade. Buildings fell and signs changed. Automobiles flashed their chrome then steel, each model different as only the most hardy of landmarks stayed the same. He refused to pay too much mind to the showcase of years, lest he would find himself lost in the spectacle. The leather shoes hit the ground and gained traction, as fast as the dawn was now chasing night and shadow. Up the hill and past the train depot that was now crumbling, strange and colorful writing on its brick. His feet hit the gravel, then the iron of the tracks. He sat down, closed his eyes, and opened them to the world he knew before, a world he would watch as a silent sentinel until the next October 31st, the same Halloween he had known for a very long time.

Invasive

Andy Lockwood

By 10 AM, Martin was on the lot of the last stocked pumpkin patch in the county. He'd started his day with his daughter's hurtful words echoing in his mind. He had let her down this Halloween season. Pumpkin hunting had been pushed back for one work meeting, then another. Before he knew it, Halloween Eve had come, and Devon was fighting tears because he'd broken his promise.

He avoided his own gaze in the rearview as he backed the car into a space in the dirt lot. Still, he could see the bags under his eyes in his peripheral vision. He looked rough. He hadn't slept well and then got up early to make sure he found a pumpkin for her. It needed to be something special.

He walked into the picked over lot, tired eyes passing over numerous pumpkins that were showing bruises and soft spots; some of them were already sagging inward. Not a single pumpkin looked good enough to take home. He'd been driving around for hours, and this was the best offering he'd found.

"Only a couple good ones left, I'm afraid." Martin turned to the sympathetic smile of a large red-faced man in dirty jeans and a flannel shirt. The man extended his hand in greeting and Martin responded in kind, watching with trepidation as his hand was swallowed up in the large fist. His thick arm was corded with veins worming beneath the surface of his skin. He gestured for Martin to follow as he walked toward the back of the produce store.

Martin sighed, holding out hope for a peace offering. He followed the broad-shouldered man around the corner, his black loafers collecting dirt and hay chaff with each step.

"We're down to these three," the man spoke. It wasn't said as an upsell, but a fact. Martin swallowed his own surprise as he saw the first of the remaining pumpkins.

It was monstrous; the largest pumpkin he'd ever seen. He barely noticed the other two beside it, squeezing out its brethren for the prize by a full foot in circumference. Swollen to bursting, its shell aglow in a mottle of fresh red, blaze orange, and midnight green. Not a single color on the pumpkin existed in nature, yet the statement immediately contradicted its own existence. Vines radiated outward from the root on top, slipping beneath the surface like tentacles. Martin couldn't help but notice the resemblance between this and the man's thick veiny arms, but shrugged off the thought as childish. The surface of the pumpkin was perfectly smooth. The striations common in pumpkins were missing. Not normally found in pumpkins were the numerous growths around the bottom. Stumps that looked like tiny stems jutted out in numerous random spots, like small legs.

Martin scratched his head, looking between the pumpkin and his compact sedan.

"Look, I don't think I can –"

"We'll deliver right to your door." It was stated with insistence, the kind that Martin felt uncomfortable arguing over. He regarded the obscene gourd again. He had no idea what he was going to do with it when Halloween was over, but he was sure Devon would be amazed by it.

Fishing out his wallet, Martin nodded, meeting the gaze of the man before him.

"How much?"

By 12 PM, Martin was standing on his sidewalk, gesturing where the pumpkin should go.

"Please tell me that's not real!" Emily called to him from the porch, her exasperation clear as she held her daughter securely. Devon was unable to stop grinning. She didn't bother to fight her mother's hold; she was too stunned by the sheer enormity of the thing being lowered off the back of the flatbed.

Two men stood on solid ground, grunting as they lowered the monstrosity as gently as they could. Two more men, including the one from the pumpkin patch, held tight to ropes that wrapped the mottled orange globe – though they struggled not to be pulled over the edge of the flatbed by the weight they tugged against.

"Oh, it's real. Every pound of it," Martin laughed, a little sheepish. He returned to the porch and made eye contact with Devon. "It's an I'm Sorry, Pumpkin." Devon groaned, but she hugged him anyway. "Thank you. It's amazing."

"How are you going to carve it?"

He hadn't considered this step in the plan, making a mental inventory of all the sharp tools in the house and garage.

"Chainsaw?"

Emily jabbed him in the arm. "You will not!"

He grinned "I might need to run to the hardware store for a saw."

By 2 PM, Martin had returned with a couple of shiny new tools that were destined to get sticky. They were certain to cut through a pumpkin, but he couldn't foresee another use for them around their suburban household. He stopped his car short of its usual spot, noting the thick vines stretching into the driveway.

Martin traced them back to the base of the pumpkin, seeing as they slithered out in all directions. They dug into the lawn, under the concrete pavers in the walkway, and snaked their way up the posts that held the porch roof aloft.

Fan-like leaves flowered at intervals and seemed to wave in an imperceptible breeze.

Martin wandered around the lawn, staring, and scratching his head. His mouth opened and closed, but no sound came out. He was amazed and could only behold the front yard with wonder.

He skirted the giant pumpkin, careful not to trip over the intricate vinery, and hopped up the stairs. Inside, Devon and Emily were sprawled out across the living room floor, organizing treat bags for all the costumed children expected to visit when the holiday observation started in earnest.

"How did you decorate the yard so fast?"

The two ladies looked up at him, then toward the front of the house, as if they might better understand the question by staring through the structure and into the yard.

"What are you talking about?" Emily's brow creased as she pushed herself to her feet. Devon hesitated, then followed behind out of curiosity.

Martin opened the door and stepped out of the way. Emily stepped through the threshold, then regarded him with surprise and suspicion.

"This is amazing." She looked between Martin and the yard, stepping across the porch to examine one vine that had begun curling around a post. "It's so lifelike."

"It really is," Martin agreed. "When did you find the time?"

"Me?" Emily looked back at him, equally in awe. "I thought you were having a laugh."

He shook his head, moving down the steps and back into the yard for another look. Emily and Devon followed, agog. Along with the intricate vine work – which appeared to be authentic – it seemed they would not need to decide on a face for the pumpkin.

It had a face of its own already.

Perhaps it wasn't a face per se, but that's what it looked like to them. The smooth surface had cracked, creating a crescent-shaped fissure along the bottom of the pumpkin. It was long and jagged, seeds and slimy pumpkin innards drooled out of the opening.

It looked hungry.

Two heavy folds of pumpkin rind rolled over the upper curve of its surface, looking very much like heavy eyebrows overstating their disapproval of the lawn it rested on.

Emily's face moved through delight into bewilderment and now rested in confusion and dismay.

"This isn't funny, Martin."

Martin looked back at her with a shrug. It hadn't been funny to begin with.

"I didn't do this."

Devon regarded her parents before turning back to the scene before them.

"Then who did?"

All the guesses they could muster defied reason.

By 4 PM, Martin watched the vines overtake the porch, sealing the doors shut. They stretched into the yard, digging deep into the lawn. Slithering further down the driveway, they'd wrapped around the front wheels and were gently sliding over, under, and through the hood of the sedan.

Devon was the one to discover that they were growing right before their eyes. She watched from the window, her phone pressed to the glass, snapping a picture every couple seconds. Eventually, she had enough photos to create a stop-motion animation of a vine climbing over the banister and wrapping itself around. It left small tendrils in its wake, anchoring itself to the path it was on.

Emily wouldn't let anyone outside to observe. It felt dangerous and made her stomach uneasy. They had an egress from the back door, out to the patio, and into the wild if they needed to leave, but she didn't feel it was safe to get near the vines. No one disagreed.

Martin searched desperately for any way to contact the farm he had gotten the pumpkin from. He could see it on the satellite map, but it wasn't labeled, providing no contact information. Did they know what they had delivered? It outpaced bamboo growth and was highly invasive.

The overgrowth had not only spread across the yard but their lives in the span of an afternoon. They spoke in whispers, afraid of the unknown lurking outside their door. Martin had only once suggested going out there with his brand-new saw to mitigate some of the damage. The look on Emily's face was enough to drop the discussion.

By 6 PM, Martin stood beside Devon at the front window, holding her close. Together, they watched costumed children on the sidewalk out front. They paused, conferring with their guardians, gawking uncertainly at the yard before continuing to the next house. It was clear to the entire neighborhood that, regardless of the lit porchlight, the owners of this house wanted no visitors.

The truth was anything but.

They tried to call for help, but the signal was being swallowed up like everything else. The pumpkin had taken over the front of the house, vines stretching from end to end of the property, pulling at the gutters and pressing against the windows. By the time Emily decided it was time to abandon their home, the mazework of vines had snuck around back and sealed off their escape.

All the windows were blocked, glass cracking loudly as the vines pressed in.

Martin pulled his family closer, humming softly as they each tried to be strong for one another, trying to block out the sounds of the house being squeezed with ever-building pressure.

By morning, Martin and his family were nowhere to be found. Though, that may have been a hasty conclusion by the police. It was the simplest explanation pieced together from the multitude of 911 calls, and the state of the property itself. To the casual observer, it appeared as if a tornado had singled out one home. That, however, was just the beginning of the mystery.

The initial investigation was slow going. No one was prepared to navigate the carpet of thick vines interwoven across the property. They set up walkways made from wooden debris and began their search, noting the slope of the property, and how the debris, as well as the tapestry of vines, rose toward the center of the lot, where the house should have been.

It took the whole day, slowly unfurling the weave work with saws and pruners. Eventually, they pulled back the curtain to reveal a swollen orange mass, the size of a trailer. Exposing more of the mass, they hoped that the family might be somewhere nearby – or perhaps even within – but the surface of the giant was smooth, unmarred except for the curved indentation that raced along to the base of the object.

There was no physical evidence that the family was here. No blood, no hair; not even a recent footprint could be found. It was like they had vanished and left behind this strange sphere in their stead.

One investigator called it a pumpkin and the name stuck. It didn't look much like a pumpkin, the resemblance stopping at round and orange. By the end of the day, they had cleared the area in question of vines. Once the crane arrived, they were able to lift the pumpkin and investigate beneath. Still, not a single clue that might lead them to the family, dead or alive.

By sunset, Martin and his family had been declared missing. Officers had been working all day alongside construction crews to uncover any evidence of the family's whereabouts. The pumpkin hung from the crane, like an unfurled yo-yo.

A large flatbed truck pulled up to the site. A large man in a flannel shirt and dirty jeans waved a clipboard at anyone who might look like they could assist. Eventually, he found a crew leader. Together, they guided the crane arm to the flatbed, where it gently lowered the pumpkin, and they strapped it down tight.

"Hell of a sight," the large man spoke quietly, removing his cap to wipe his brow. "Any leads?"

The red face offered a sympathetic smile, but the crew leader only shook his head. "They've got nothing."

They stood together for another minute in respectful silence, then the broad-shouldered man grunted his departure. The crew leader extended his hand, watching with surprise as his hand disappeared within the larger fist. He looked up the thick arm, his heavy brow furrowing at the veins that shifted beneath the skin.

The crew leader watched the descending sun cast long shadows across the truck as it eased back onto the road. He took a long last look at the pumpkin, noting how un-pumpkin-like it truly was. The intense orange rays made the pumpkin glow brighter, the crew leader squinting against the unnatural intensity. He watched the flatbed turn down the next street and, as the sun traced shadows on every imperfection of the orange sphere, the shadows made it look like the pumpkin was smiling.

Thinking of You

Jenifer Lynn

James' hands clenched around the baby blue steering wheel of Mr. Thomason's brand new 1954 Chevy Bel Air. The finger grips were set too far apart and hurt his fingers. A steady stream of mumbled curses slipped through his gritted teeth as he tried to find the right pressure on the gas pedal with his right foot without riding too hard on the break with his left.

The game of Halloween dares had gone too far. Lying under train trestles was one thing, and Pauly hadn't even been hurt too bad. And all Billy had to do was run across the football field in his skivvies, and it wasn't like anyone was there this late at night. Having to take the principal's brand new car out for a joy ride was *way* worse. *Way* worse, and not at all fair. He wasn't even old enough to drive for real yet.

He pushed his left foot down as the intersection of Grand Avenue and Church Road appeared in the headlights. He was halfway there. Two more right turns and two more long, dark country roads and he'd have the car back in Mr. Thomason's driveway. Then Billy and Pauly wouldn't be able to call him a chicken.

The car slowed to a crawl as he cranked the giant steering wheel to the right, turning onto Church Road. This road was twisty, and hilly, and dark even when the sun was out. Old trees grew tall and shaded the packed gravel that served as asphalt this far from town. The Chevy's headlamps did little to dissipate the blackness, and James hesitated to push down his right foot much at all, creeping along the winding path.

Five minutes later he was starting to feel more comfortable. A clearing opened up in the trees and the town church appeared at the top of the next hill. That meant that there was just one more bend before a two mile straight shot to the next intersection. He slowed down to take the turn in front of the church, then slammed both feet on the brake pedal. The Chevy came to an abrupt stop, kicking up a cloud of dust that rushed into the headlights, temporarily obscuring the young woman who stood in the middle of the lane.

Frozen, he watched her as she turned to look at the car. She was dressed for the holiday, a costume party, with a fancy 1920s dress that had dangling, glittering beads, pale legs showing from the knee down. Her hair, a deep mahogany, was done up in the waves that had been the fashion when his mother was just a child. She wore long necklaces, and a sparkling barrette in her hair to match. Her face was shaped like a heart, eyes huge and blue that locked with his for just a moment before they seemed to glaze over, sliding past him.

He sat up straight, barely able to see over the dash, and rolled his window down. "Did you need a ride?" he called to her. He scrambled across the console to lift up the lock on the passenger side.

She nodded slowly and moved to the door without a word, opening it, the beads of her dress clacking together as she sat down and shut the door. She stared out the windshield as the dust finally dissipated.

"So..." James said. "Where are we going?"

She turned to look at him, her red lips parting to softly say, "Home."

James nodded, taking one foot off the brake pedal. The car jolted into motion when he hit the gas, and he laughed nervously. "So, where is home?"

The woman kept her eyes on the road in front of them, not answering.

"That way?" he asked.

Again, she was silent.

James swallowed hard, trying to keep his eyes on the road, though a big part of him wanted to keep looking at the woman. She was the most beautiful thing he'd ever seen, and he had seen three Grace Kelly movies that year, so he knew a lot about beautiful women.

He kept driving until he saw the stop sign where Church ended at Clark Valley Road. He looked down at his feet, making sure his left was on the brake pedal before he slowly stepped down, easing the car to a stop a few yards short of the intersection.

"Which way is-" He turned back to the passenger seat, words failing when he saw there was no one there.

"What the...?" He threw the car into park and turned himself around, searching the empty back seat, then squinting to see out the back window. The tail lights cast a red glow on clouds of dust and a barren road.

James sat there, searching, for a long time before he finally put the car in drive and made his last right turn before his dare was accomplished and the principal's car would be returned.

***

James made his twentieth turn onto Church Road since the sun had set. The car he drove was far less extravagant than the one he'd had the year previous, an old Ford that his father had bought when he came home from the war.

He made the turns down the dark road with greater ease now, having gotten his driving permit that summer, and having practiced on this road specifically many times since. He held his breath for the twentieth time as he rounded the last bend before the straightaway.

She was there. Finally. Standing still in the headlights. Exactly as she had been a year ago.

"I knew it!" he exclaimed, slamming the brakes and rolling down his window, muttering, "Pauly and Billy can eat dirt. I knew she would be here." He stuck his head out the window. "Hey, nice to see you again. Can I give you a ride?"

She turned to him, nodding, and moved to the door, just as she had last Halloween. The beads in her dress clattered against each other. The smell of her perfume, lilac, floated pleasantly in the cab. "I knew you'd be here," he said to her. "I looked and looked for days till I realized it was probably because it was Halloween."

She turned her large blue eyes to him and blinked. Her blank stare faltering for a moment.

"Do you remember me?" he asked. "I'm James. I picked you up last year." He sat up straight, his height now plenty to see over the dash. "I was a lot smaller then, though, so maybe you don't..."

She had turned her gaze back to the road in front of them.

"Okay, so..." he breathed. "I guess we'll just drive for a bit."

He let off the brake and the car stuttered to life, moving down the straightaway.

James continued talking, "It's about midnight, isn't it? Maybe that's the trick. You show up at midnight on Halloween?" He shook his head, unable to keep his focus on the road ahead, worried that he would lose her again. "I wish I'd known that before I spent weeks walking up and down that road."

"I saw you," she said softly. Her eyes still trained forward.

"What?" he asked. "You saw me on the road?"

But she had fallen silent again, blank.

He kept his eyes on her as they reached the stop sign at the end of Church, slowing to a crawl. She was still the most beautiful thing he'd ever seen, and he had seen Marilyn Monroe in The Seven Year Itch that summer. This woman sitting next to him was even more beautiful than Marilyn Monroe. He wanted to say that to her. That would be a nice thing for a girl to hear.

He opened his mouth to speak, stopping short. She was starting to fade, the door handle beside her clearly showing through her translucent torso. She turned to him, focusing on him for a moment. He thought that maybe she smiled just before she disappeared. But he couldn't be sure.

He circled around Church Road twenty more times that night before finally going home.

***

The boy was sitting on a rock. Though less of a boy now than he had been the last time she saw him. Broader in the shoulders, and taller. He sat on a rock at the edge of the woods and flicked the ashes from a cigarette, eyes scanning the road. He had been there for a while, she thought, though time had little meaning for her anymore.

His gaze finally landed on her and he smiled. "I was worried you wouldn't show up if I didn't bring my ride," he said. He stood, closing the distance between them. "Can I walk with you?"

She had to get home. Down the straight road. The urge like a heavy fog enveloped her and she began walking. He walked beside her, feet crunching on the gravel, cigarette smoke swirling around them as he talked.

Her attention faded in and out as he told her about his year. As he talked, she felt the fog lift slightly, as it had the last times she'd seen him. Pauly and Billy still didn't believe him about her, so he didn't tell them where he was going when he left the Halloween party. It was boring anyway. He hadn't dressed up, because didn't want to confuse her. He figured she would recognize him better if he wasn't dressed up like the Wolfman or something. And speaking of movies, he had seen...

His words faded again, the pull forward high jacking her fragmented thoughts. The road ahead narrowed as though squeezed into a tube. Gravel. Leaves. Wind. Cold. Dark. A fast approaching stop sign.

"Hey." The boy appeared in her tunneled vision, leaning down to meet her at eye level. "Hey, I lost you there, I think." He smiled, a wide, kind smile.

Her vision snapped open like a rubber band, expanding almost too big before contracting back. The world around her normalized, solidified, and became real once again. At the center of it, was the boy.

"James," she said, her voice almost startling her.

His smile, impossibly, grew wider.

"Yes! I'm James!" His smile faltered. "Wait, please don't go."

But she felt it. The fog was closing in again. The long fog. The one from which she couldn't possibly pull free.

"Please, stay," he said, voice suddenly very far away. "At least tell me your name before you disappear again."

But then her world was gray and shifting shadows, and James was gone.

***

"June."

Her soft, whispered voice jolted James from a near-doze. He stood from his rock and spun around to see her. His memory never did her justice, and the pleasant flutter in his stomach when he saw her had only grown stronger as he got older. For the first time, her eyes seemed clear before he spoke to her, watching him closely. He suddenly felt self-conscious, uncomfortably aware that his t-shirt and work pants were covered in mud. He scrubbed at the grime with dirt-covered palms.

"June?" he said.

"M-my... name," she spoke haltingly, as though it was a struggle to get the words out.

James took a deep breath, abandoning his futile attempt to look presentable. "It is so nice to meet you June."

***

James continued meeting her, year after year. It got easier for her to fight off the fog during their long midnight walks, but she was unable to stop her trajectory, and once they reached the crossroads, she would inevitably fade.

Nevertheless, they made use of their time together. Talking, laughing, and telling stories. June was 22 years old. Or had been. Or still was. She never spoke of what brought her to Church Road, and he never pushed to find out.

She had been a music teacher, and a singer. It took him three years to convince her to sing for him, and when she finally did, a soulful song called "I'll Be Blue Just Thinking of You", he knew he was never going to love anyone like he loved her. He had tried to touch her that night. Reaching out for her as they walked.

There was nothing there. His hand passed through her fingers. She had brought her hand to her chest, her large blue eyes shining as she blinked away tears. That Halloween, the rest of the walk had been quiet, and she didn't look at him when she faded away.

***

The fade from gray to the real world was jarring. June found herself almost stumbling as the illusion of hard ground beneath her connected with her feet. The sensation had grown stronger, stranger, since she'd met James.

Stronger still was the rock in her stomach at the memory of their last night. His expression when he found he was unable to touch her had broken her heart. She was certain that he wouldn't show again. Certain that he had grown old enough to want more than just their long walks. He would be her age by now.

When he wasn't on his rock, June felt the world fade, slipping away again as her feet began their yearly journey.

Sadness and anger pulled her from the tunnel in increments along her path, painting the road in stark contrast to the fog beyond.

She was a third of the way to the crossroads when headlights fell on her, and a honk shocked her back into focus. With not a small amount of struggle, she made herself stop and turn. The headlights were too bright to allow her to see anything beyond, but she could hear his voice.

"June!" he called to her. The door opened and slammed shut. "June, I'm so sorry I'm late."

Her feet wanted to move, but she stayed planted, waiting for him to reach her. He had grown to his full height a few years previous. A job in construction had filled out his chest and shoulders, making his silhouette imposing against the bright headlights.

"Please forgive me, June," he said. "I was planning a surprise for you and it took too long."

"I have to go," June said, her feet turning in the gravel.

"Wait," he moved in front of her so she could see his face. He was dressed up this time, a pinstripe suit straight out of her era. "At least let me drive you. Slowly." He smiled at her. "We can listen to music."

Music. The idea of music swayed her, loosening her feet and allowing her to move backward to get into his car. The radio was playing softly as she settled into the passenger seat, and James turned the button to make it louder. A brass band played background to a clarinet player in a short but exciting instrumental number before a man's voice broke in at the end, announcing the name of the band and song title.

June opened her mouth to say she enjoyed it, but James put his finger to his lips. "Listen to him," he said.

"This young man has his holidays mixed around, but he was very insistent that he be allowed to dedicate a song to his lady love tonight," the man was saying. "Why this old song, you may ask? Well why Halloween, would be my answer. So June, I hope you're listening, because your beau James slid me a lot of dough to play this one. This is 'I'll be Blue Just Thinking of You'."

The music started again, and June's voice joined the vocalist on cue, "I'm walking 'round in circles, trying to forget," shyly she glanced at James as she continued singing, "that I ever fell in love with you. I'm walking 'round in circles ever since we met. What else is there left for me to do?"

The car slowed to a stop and James got out, moving around to the passenger side and opening her door and holding out his hand. Her singing trailed off. "But I..."

"Dance with me, June," he said. "We can pretend."

She hesitated, then reached out, laying her hand atop his. There was no resistance, but she held her hand there and stood, following his lead as he pulled her away from the car and into an embrace that she couldn't feel. He began to sway from side to side, singing off-key to the upcoming verse, "I thought we'd play a while. Forget to say goodbye."

She relented, swaying with him. "Don't sing anymore," she said, a hint of a laugh.

"Am I that terrible?" he asked.

"The lyrics are too sad for you to sing," she said, following along as he mimed spinning her under their raised arms. "And you're terrible."

He laughed, pulling her back to him. Her feet moved easily with him, the pull toward the end of the road forgotten for the duration of their dance. And the next dance. And the next.

***

Eventually the songs were replaced by a radio play, and the spell was broken. June began her walk to the crossroads, and James followed, leaving his car running in the street behind them.

"Thank you for tonight, James," she said.

He felt like he could have danced with her till dawn, and wondered if there was a way to bring more music next time. "We can do it again next year!"

"No," she said, looking down at the ground and shaking her head. "No, I don't want to do this again."

"But, I thought you had fun," he said, his mood falling fast from its precipice.

"I did," she said. "But I worry that maybe you think there's more here than what there is."

His stomach twisted. "What do you mean?" he turned to her. "June, I love-"

She held up a hand, cutting him off. "Don't," she said. "It's silly. Just don't." She wouldn't look at him, attention focused on the stop sign a few yards ahead, her steps coming faster. His own feet wouldn't move, rooted to the ground where his heart had dropped. "Don't come back next year, James." She reached the crossroads and turned to look at him as she began to fade. "Don't come back at all."

***

"I know why you did it."

His voice startled her from her walk and she turned, swallowing the emotion that welled up. There had been seven lonely Halloweens since she last saw him. Long walks in silence and sadness, slipping in and out of the world.

He looked older, but not old. His hair was cut shorter and styled. Dress slacks and a blazer, the clothes of a respectable adult. He reached in his jacket pocket, pulling out his wallet. "I didn't get it then, but I do now, and I hope you'll let me walk with you tonight, so I can thank you."

She nodded, allowing him to catch up to her. He pulled something from his wallet and turned it so she could see. It was an image of two children, a boy of maybe five, and a toddler girl. Both smiled at the camera, dressed in their Sunday best. "Their names are Bobby and Mary June."

June's eyes widened.

"Isn't she the most beautiful girl you've ever seen?" James chuckled. "She wouldn't have been born if you hadn't shooed me away, so I thought she should have your name, at least a little." He pulled out another picture. "Not that I told my wife where I got the name. She thinks I'm a respectable husband and I don't want to tip her off in any way."

The second image was a wedding picture. James the groom beamed, and his bride, a small blonde woman, was glowing. June felt a bittersweet wave flow through her. "You're happy?"

"I'm happy," he said. "Thanks to you." He put his wallet away, falling into step next to her. "I would have walked and danced with you for the rest of my life if you'd've let me."

She smiled sadly, "You deserved better than that."

He was quiet for a moment, then spoke up again, hesitant. "Can I tell you about my kids?"

She laughed, surprising both of them. "I would love to hear about your kids."

***

In the years that followed, he never missed a Halloween with June. He told her about the kids, their antics and their grades. He reenacted the moon landing for her, as she laughed in disbelief. She sat quiet with him as he told her about how his brother-in-law had been lost in the war. A few Halloweens later, she kindly pretended not to notice his tears as he told her about the divorce. His pride was tangible when he told her about his daughter graduating high school as valedictorian, moreso when she got her college degree. And she cooed with him over the baby pictures of his first grandchild. Every great once in a while, they would turn up the radio and dance.

***

"June, I brought some music," James said one night as she got into his car. She had lost track of how many nights they'd spent together, but time had made itself known. His handsome face was wrinkled, laugh lines deep in his cheeks. His hair, now gray and thin, was slicked back the way he'd been wearing it for decades. Worn and wrinkled fingers held up a plastic box. "This is a cassette tape that I made just for you," he said, fiddling with the console. A moment later her song began to play.

"Will you dance with me, June?" he asked. "One more time?"

He got out of the car, moving slowly around to open her door. She frowned at him. "What do you mean 'one more time'?"

He held out his hand. "I'm old," he said. "I'm not sure how many more Halloweens I have left, let alone ones where my kids'll let me take my midnight drive. Let us have this before I'm too feeble-bodied and addle-brained."

June hovered her hand above his and stepped out of the car. She wanted to protest that he wasn't old, that that would never happen, but he would know it was a lie. Her stomach ached a little as they started their dance, slower than it had been on that first night. She could see that it hurt him to move like that anymore, a stutter in his steps when he shifted the wrong way. But he smiled at her through that dance and the next, spinning her around through the third before he finally relented and led them back to the car.

They talked the rest of the night, ignoring the push of movement, of morning, for as long as they could. They talked as though it were any other night, ignoring that it would be their last. When she heard birdsong for the first time since she had died, there was a heartbeat of hope that maybe whatever powers had forced her into this never ending loop had finally taken mercy on her.

But cruelly, the fog moved in as it always had, and she was unable to blink back her tears as she turned to James for the last time. His eyes were shining as well, and he put his hand on top of hers, through hers. "June," he said as the fog closed in around them. "I love you."

When the fog lifted again, the birdsong was silent and June was alone.

***

It didn't take long before her nights bled into one another once again. The new contrast of loneliness pulled her hard and fast away from recognizing time as it passed. Just the endless walk, the crunch of gravel, the tunnel vision to the distant stop sign. She knew it would happen, over and over, forever, so she just stopped fighting it.

***

"Is it possible to dance with no music?"

June blinked, remembering the voice.

"I could sing, maybe?" the voice continued, clearing away the mists that surrounded her. "But I've been told I'm terrible."

A figure stood to her left. She saw his silhouette first, tall and broad, before he came into focus, his features handsome and youthful. His name flickered around her mind, hesitant to hope.

"James?" she whispered.

He smiled, a bright, kind smile, and slipped his hand into hers, his palm was warm and rough. His fingers threaded with hers and he squeezed, releasing the memories she had pushed away. A lifetime of Halloweens came flooding back, solidifying the world around her, and solidifying him.

"So..." James said. "Where are we going?"

She looked up at him, smiling before she softly answered, "Home."

The Tunnel

Jess Boldt

Another Halloween, and we're back at Memorial Park. Well, *we* were until *they* decided to go into the tunnel, like it's some tradition. Just because you get stuck in a loop of stupidity doesn't mean that it's a tradition. Yet here I am, another Halloween, sitting in a beat up car that smells of cigarettes and trash. Tradition, no, just the type of thing that bored kids with no money find themselves doing over and over again. Trevor, Jakey, and myself, every year. We'd park our bikes at this secluded gravel lot where the couples from school come after every lame dance for some heavy petting and beyond. All this so the boy can shout his accomplishments in the locker room before Coach Brames comes in and shuts it down, often with an approving smile. The whole ritual of it all is disgusting.

But every year, we come back. Been doing it since we were old enough to peddle past the tracks and into the rich area. We'd speed past the kids going door to door, holding out their bags for full-sized candy bars and the occasional toothbrush. Trevor wore the same skeleton mask he wore every year, although it looks sort of stupid on his wide face these days. Jakey never grew out of his hooded ghost mask, but the poor kid never really grew. And I'm sitting in this car, holding my latex ghoul mask in my lap. It still fits well enough after all these years, but I don't know if I fit it anymore. I guess that's why they're in the tunnel and I'm out here, freezing my balls off.

The tunnel. A ribbed length of aluminum that protrudes from the side of a hill just below a road lined with wealthy houses with perfect lawns. The first year we decided to go into the sewers, at least we have always assumed it was the sewers because the only exits besides the tunnel entrance were scattered manholes, we were looking for something to do besides trick-or-treat. We had heard stories from the older kids about this place. Mostly BS to scare younger kids, but I guess they intrigued us at the time. The first time we went in, I thought Jakey was going to piss himself, for real. We told him to go for it, cause it was, after all, the sewers. Poor guy steeled his nerves to make it into the tunnel proper. A few rooms in and past the broken beer bottles, we came upon a room filled with lewd graffiti and baby dolls that someone hung from the ceiling with string and crazy glue. I have to admit, it was impressive, we felt like we had pushed ourselves into something not quite meant for us yet.

That was the thing about that tunnel, the labyrinth inside was a real freakshow. Teenagers have been coming down here for years to drink, smoke dope, and spray paint every inch of grey concrete they could. Nothing profound, just a bunch of dicks and edgy satan shit like '666' and poorly drawn pentagrams. Sometimes there would be song lyrics that some moron thought defined them. Jesus, can you imagine someone defined by "Pour some sugar on me" or "I'll just end up walkin' in the cold November rain?". And when they got really bored or felt really motivated, they would decorate the tunnels. Baby dolls splashed with red paint. Some ambitious asshole brought a mannequin down and stuck a dull knife in its hand. That hokey doll made Jakey piss himself for real, although he never did admit it.

Trevor, fuck Trevor. Now that he's the one with the car, he gets to choose what we do, and he isn't too nice about it. My arm still hurts from the punch he gave me when I said we're too old for this shit. I guess that's why I didn't go this time. I'm just sick of it. I didn't go in, yeah, why would I think that. I've been sitting here for over an hour now. Although I was tempted when Jakey mocked me, calling me a pussy for not doing something I've done year after year. I guess he's been waiting for the chance to be the big guy and took it. I can't blame him for that. I can blame him for smacking the back of my head as he left the car. After all the times I've stepped in when Trevor was going on a manic tear. Took more than a few punches for him. Lately he's been emulating Trevor at his worst times, the times the meds wore off or he just refused to take them. I heard Jakey even threatened his sister with a knife the other day. Sure, it was a goddamn butter knife, but still, just another example of him trying to pry his way out of his lot in life. At least the cops weren't called when he did it, not like when Trevor held an actual knife to his dad. That was a mess. And if he would of stuck his dad, the abusive fucker would have had it coming. It would have been doing him a favor really, snuffing out something that had become rotten over the years. The same rot that had infected Trevor, that was infecting... Jesus it's cold.

Maybe that's why I had to, I had to wait in this car. How long have I been waiting? An hour? We never went in for this long. They're probably sipping on a beer Jakey snuck away or something. But they have to be coming out soon. But they aren't coming out, are they? No, of course they are. They wouldn't leave me out here, after all, Trevor wouldn't leave his car for some prank, even if he didn't pop a pill this morning. And Jakey? Sure, he's getting mouthy but he wouldn't stay down there this long, no matter the perceived status it would give him.

Alright, I just need some music, well, the radio would be nice but Trevor took his keys with him. Of course he did. Wouldn't let me waste his precious gas for some warmth and entertainment. His keys, probably in his pocket right now, just laying there next to his pocket knife. But the knife isn't in his pocket, is it? The same knife he flashed in front of my face in the school bathroom last week. I don't think he's taken his meds for weeks now. And that's why it's okay he's not coming out. That's why he's lying face down with his neck open wide.

Christ, what's going on? Am I trying to freak myself out? Probably, no radio. Halloween night. Sure, just a bad thought in lieu of the radio or conversation, or even heat. But what if I did that? I could have. I could have just walked in minutes after them. Jumped him. We would wrestle but his guard would have been down. And that's why the knife isn't in his pocket, is it? I would have taken it out in the faux struggle, then when his back was turned, a quick release followed by a quick motion across his neck. He would move around, oblivious to what just happened, then pure shock.

Okay, this isn't fun. I didn't kill anyone and I certainly didn't kill my friend, no matter how much of a bastard he's been. Not his fault really, his family, his broken brain, I wouldn't do that to a friend. I have to breathe and just relax. For fuck sake, that doesn't even make sense. Jakey would be losing his head right now, screaming and running around the park until he dropped. And that would bring attention.

Sure, for a few seconds he would stand there, not believing his own eyes which reflected Trevor's wide, stunned eyes as the blood began to soak his black sweater. And in that instance, a choice had to be made. A choice that didn't allow debate, but quick action, the rot had infected him as well. A quick motion into his small body to throw off his balance. A small squeak as the air left his lungs. Six, maybe seven, thrusts into the chest, some more difficult than others. Back off, careful not to get the blood on my hands. Too late, but just the hands. Wash them off in the small stream of cold October water below my feet. Wash the knife handle off as well. Go back to the car... and, and seriously, stop. I need to stop this. Is this what the rot feels like?

I didn't kill anyone, I wouldn't. I just couldn't. They're coming out, any minute now. Any second now. They are going to come out of that tunnel, and everything is going to be okay. Would it be okay? Have things been okay? Of course not, or I wouldn't have... I have to get out of this car. I'm driving myself nuts. Some fresh air. Good idea, get out of the car. Say you waited for them and you just decided to walk home, even if it means that you have to say you were too much of a pussy to go in. Never admit I set one foot in that tunnel. Never. But I never did. Exactly.

No, I'm done with this stupid game, even if I'm the only one playing. I'm just going to walk a little closer to the tunnel. Away from that car. Why am I still holding this stupid mask? Maybe because it's better if I put it on, just in case a car passes. It's Halloween, nobody would think twice about a ghoul walking around the park, but some stupid teen, that's something those rich assholes would call the cops on. But why would that matter, I didn't do anything wrong I just, I just need to sit down. Sit on that stump and calm down. That's better, I can wait and watch through these holes cut into this latex. I guess it does fit me, rather I fit it.

It doesn't matter, I'm wearing it now. And they're going to walk out of that tunnel at any moment and I'll let a long sigh of relief, wave to them and never mention this stupid mind game to anyone. But will I feel relief or a small pang of disappointment? If they don't come out, then what? If they do, then what? I have no idea how I'll feel, regardless of what happens. And that is scaring the hell out of me.

A Dish Served
Cold

Andy Lockwood

Leaves tumbled down the empty street, the last travelers having vanished for home hours earlier. Streetlights cast a fitting orange glow over everything in their reach. Porch lights shut off one by one as little goblins and witches ran the houses out of candy. For what was a thriving, churning mass a short time ago, the neighborhood now felt barren.

This was the time when all the excitement moved indoors. Children dumped their treasure troves over the living room floor as they sat with their parents, each separating good candy from bad, both having very different definitions of each.

October was slowly easing out into the night, welcoming November with quiet resignation. In a few short hours, the neighborhood would wake up and start discussing the pros and cons of leaving the decorations up till the weekend. But in one yard, tucked among the ghosts and zombies, a shadow sat straighter than any others, disturbingly still in the breeze that rolled around it.

Marty Sandoval ignored the cold that seeped into his knees almost an hour ago. He'd come home with a ruined costume and a bruise on his left cheek from where he'd been punched. His parents tried to console him, but there was nothing left to say. Marty was all too used to this treatment – not just on Halloween but throughout the year. He'd been the subject of scorn and torment from elementary school on.

"They'll grow out of it eventually," his parents promised. He'd taken solace in their wisdom initially, but time had proven that his bullies were more dedicated to tradition than his parents gave them credit for. Marty's hope was slowly worn away, like his joy for school – or leaving the house at all. A darkness swallowed up the laughter that used to come easily, and from it, something new blossomed.

Anger burned like a molten core within him. It was a new feeling, one that Marty was not sure he liked. At times, it felt like strength; but other times, its jagged points turned inward and hurt him as much as he could hurt anyone else. He tried to stuff it back down, but it fed on everything else within him, all-consuming and burning brighter.

He knew he should find a way to let it go. Anger led to hate, and hate to suffering, it was said. He wasn't sure that was a path he wanted to take, but then Halloween came.

Halloween was supposed to be good scares and fun costumes and laughter. Marty had worked for a whole month on his robot costume, all shimmering aluminum and flashing lights. But the laughter vanished when Josh and his lackeys pulled onto Mansion Street.

Marty wasn't sure how three boys not much bigger than him gathered so much power and control to them. Anyone dumb enough to stand up to them was pummeled quickly. Marty knew he wasn't the only one, but it wasn't exactly the club he wanted to belong to.

Josh led Carl and Rocky down the middle of the street, watching as the crowd parted around them. On occasion, they'd grab someone's candy bag – or someone altogether – and give them the piñata treatment. Marty and his friends hadn't been anywhere near the line of fire; they couldn't have recognized him through the giant robot head. It was a combination of sheer dumb luck and looking breakable.

Josh's eyes lit up light Christmas morning when he pulled the robot mask off and revealed Marty's glowering scowl. Marty knew he was the treat to Josh's trick. The anger welled up predictably, heat coloring his vision as he swung the plastic pumpkin. The satisfying weight of his candy hoard connected solidly with Josh's face before anyone knew what was happening. Marty's friends wasted no time disappearing into the crowd – he could hardly blame them – he would have done the same. Carl and Rocky could only stare, a mixture of horror and fear crossed their stunned faces. Josh only lost a moment before he dropped his bike and threw a punch that took Marty off his feet.

It hurt. It was hard to find words with that much pain

swirling in his skull. His vision popped in white flashes, then darkened, obliterating the view of the sidewalk rushing up at him. All three bullies descended on him, shredding his hard work all around him, then moving further up the block to ruin someone else's night.

Marty lay on the sidewalk, costumed revelers parting around him, actively ignoring him as he collected himself to go home. He didn't know how long he stayed there, staring hot and angry into the imperfections along the walkway. It was less of picking himself up and more that he shoved himself to his feet. He was a bundle of taut sinew and fiery rage. A sensation that did not release him when he got home.

Staring at his front door, he knew what waited: coddling and condolences, while the humiliation and pain seeped into his skin like sunburn. On the other hand, there were several things in the garage that might help him ease his turmoil – or at least distract him from the pain.

***

They rode slowly, making wide serpentine arcs down the street. They were the last of the revelers, refusing to call it a night until they had expended every last drop of Halloween mischief. One shadowy rider pointed the others toward the only house on the block that still beckoned with lights and decorations. Witches and ghosts dangling from tree limbs drifted lazily in the breeze. Tombstones tilted and leaned, some held up by skeletal hands reaching out of the dirt. The whole yard was bathed in purple, green, and red light. More than two dozen jack-o-lanterns glowed brightly across the yard and along the walkway, calling the boys like a siren song. Marty held his breath, tucked into his hiding spot; the fire within him bubbled.

Carl was first, letting his bike drop in the street as he lumbered into the yard. He was an ogre; wide uncertain steps and huffing breath heralded his arrival. He paused in front of the jack-o-lanterns Marty had stolen from neighboring houses. Various levels of artistry were on display across the yard. Pumpkins big and small were organized in slapdash patterns – it was all Marty could devise on such short notice. Where Carl stood, a tempting pyramid of Halloween faces flickered back at him.

A grin split his face but there was no mirth behind it, only malice. He peered at the glowing mountain from beneath a hefty shelf of forehead. Grabbing the top pumpkin in his meaty fists, the tower wobbled, threatening to topple. Marty had arranged the pumpkins with the barest structural integrity in mind. It was enough to keep them balanced atop one another. It was a lure, not a display.

As expected, Carl hefted the top pumpkin, his breathing louder and faster as he labored. The other two boys were just crossing the sidewalk, flicking kickstands as

Carl's pumpkin rose high in the night, glowing uncertainly as he shook the prize his hands.

Marty watched breathlessly from the darkness; his fists clenched in anticipation of the pumpkin splintering on the lawn. Instead, he was surprised to see his haphazard plans flounder in spectacular fashion.

To anyone else bearing witness, the interior of the jack-o-lantern guttered out momentarily. Then, as quickly as it vanished, the glow returned, erupting in brilliant yellow fire. It lit the neighborhood as flame belched and flared from the pumpkin's hollowed features. Carl, clearly startled, let the pumpkin fall. It turned in the air, twisting around and landing with a solid thud on its back. The impact split the joyful pumpkin face, fire arcing up around Carl as the shell spit fiery hell.

Marty covered his mouth and ogled. He didn't know if he was horrified or delighted. He felt his eyes bulge further as he watched the flames spread. They spread hungrily over Carl, moving in endless waves as they consumed his cheap plastic costume. Carl smacked the flames fruitlessly, each passing moment becoming more desperate. His arms whirled as he screamed, only seeming to feed the flames as he stumbled blindly, fire rising, clinging to his meaty frame. Arms whirling, body twisting, the ox threw himself off balance and pitched into the pyramid, disappearing within the pile as it toppled over on him.

There was a moment of silence as Carl hit the ground, then an unholy sound as a half dozen water balloons filled with gasoline burst inside the other pumpkins and immediately fed the wildfire overtaking him. A tower of fire exploded from the center of the broken pyramid, halting the two boys who had run to help. The screaming continued; a flailing blaze struggled to find its feet, crawling on hands and knees, before collapsing once more.

Eventually, the figure that used to be Carl stopped thrashing. In fact, it stopped moving altogether. The other two boys could only stare as the fire continued to flicker and crackle. A smell – something acrid yet sweet – drifted on the air. It made Marty think of roasting hot dogs and blackened marshmallows.

Marty watched the street with curiosity, surprised that not a single porch light had lit. Sure, the fire had gone quickly, but Carl was loud. Still, no one interrupted the scene.

"What was that?" Rocky started, tugging at his hair in panic. "Carl? You okay?"

The fist came out of nowhere. Josh caught Rocky square in the jaw. Marty watched Rocky stumble, almost dropping into a pool of flame.

"He's on fire – do you think he's okay?"

Marty stifled a laugh. No one knew he was here. As the boys argued, Marty reached down and flipped the switch on the power strip. A small red glow came to life; the witches and ghosts followed.

The argument died instantly; Rocky and Josh looked at each other, then back at the figures that zoomed around the yard at head height. Witches zigged; ghosts zagged. The boys remained somewhere in the middle.

"Who's doing this?" Josh yelled; his head on a swivel. He stomped into the foam graveyard, picking up a dollar store headstone and throwing it at the house. It sailed far, but only lightly tapped the window before disappearing into the bushes. He kicked another headstone, watching as it sailed across the lawn. Josh backed up to kick another, stepping onto the grave blanket that lay before each headstone.

Marty wondered if, somewhere in Josh's mind, he knew what was about to happen. It was too dark to see the moment of realization as Josh's foot triggered the release on the bear trap.

Josh fell to the ground, his voice cracking with fear as pain and panic overwhelmed him. Rocky backed up, his eyes darting all around, ignoring his friend's whimpering pleas for help. Rocky took a single step forward, then shuffled back again, clearly afraid of what was to come.

The fear blinded him. He was blind to the tension line bouncing right in front of him until it was too late. A ghost floated through the yard, pulled along the wire route, and snuck up from his flank. It floated into his peripheral vision one moment, his face the next. The cheesecloth ghost clung to his face; its form wet and clingy. Rocky tugged at the fabric, tossing it away without another thought until his sinuses reacted.

His nose and eyes started running, then burning. He pawed desperately at his face, trying to wipe his eyes clean. His distress only served to spread the pepper spray around, rubbing it into every open pore. Within a minute, his eyes were swollen shut, his nostrils choked with snot. He rasped open-mouthed, unable to wipe his hands clean fast enough. He rubbed them on his thighs, trying again to clear his face. Out of context, it was a silly dance; Marty mused that he should have brought a camera.

Rocky spun and sputtered as he fanned his arms, a pitiful impression of Frankenstein's Monster. The pain and blindness held him to a general area, still very much in the path of the floating decorations as they flit down the wire path. The witch crumpled against his shoulder, its vinyl dress crinkling loudly. Rocky grabbed one striped stocking leg and wrenched the lifeless form away.

It was the right move; the same choice anyone might make in his situation. But one strong tug was all Rocky needed to know he'd chosen poorly. The darkness – and chemically-assisted blindness – masked the dozens of fishhooks and razor blades that swirled around the witch as she flew around the yard. Had Rocky encountered the witch before the ghost, he might have noticed all the sharp bits that hung around him like glitter. Instead, he pulled, and hooks anchored; razor blades cut into his palm and his arm, slashing as he tried to pull himself free of his distress. Marty watched the back and forth, wondering how long Rocky would continue to hurt himself before calming down and assessing his trouble.

Rocky was clearly not the type to calm down and assess. Instead, the lines got tighter, the hooks pulled harder, and his skin strained against thin wire. His only relief from the burning in his senses was the hot wash of blood from numerous cuts and piercings. Exhausted, he gave out and collapsed; he rasped long and rough, rattling in the night the line attached to him pulled taut, suspending him inches above the ground.

Madness descended on Josh, whirling and rebounding from every shadow, every flicker of light. One friend smoldered on the lawn, the other was partly suspended, floundering and possibly suffocating. Still, Josh didn't make a move toward either. Fear – and a bear trap – kept him from taking a step in any direction.

"I wasn't sure I could actually do it," Marty clenched his fists, digging his fingernails into his palms. The pain distracted him from his own fear and kept the shaking in his voice to a minimum.

"Marty?" The word came out in a stammer. There was the barest recognition in Josh's eyes as he looked around the yard, finally returning his gaze to his longtime punching bag. "What did you do?"

"Technically, nothing." He breathed deeply, the mixture of cool autumn air mixing with the smell of the burning lawn. "You're trespassing. I was never here."

"But why?" It was like Josh hadn't caught up yet. His brain stalled; it couldn't process what it'd seen.

"Why? Really? You're going to ask me why?"

Josh took a step, then dropped to a knee again, groaning. There was a sharp blink, like invisible fingers snapping in Josh's face, and then he was awake, alert, and angry.

"I'm going to kill you, you little turd!"

Ignoring the obvious impediment, Josh covered the distance in a matter of steps. Desperate strides made up for Marty's short backward shuffling – unfortunately, Josh did not learn from his friends' misfortune.

His good foot came down on the lawn and kept going. Damp grass and brown leaves sprang up comically as the cardboard buckled and his foot slid into the hole. He grunted as his foot hit the bottom and his ankle twisted. His other knee bent, bringing him to rest uncomfortably on the bear trap wrapped around his other foot.

Marty was surprised that pain sounded so different

from what he heard in movies. It was less frustration and depth of voice and more high-pitched desperation and fear. It surprised him; he'd built up his bully subconsciously – he was a little surprised to find that Josh wasn't actually invincible.

Josh pawed desperately at the metal trap beneath him. He howled; a concoction of terror and pain. Marty winced at the sound but carried on.

He lugged the gas can, still surprised how much five gallons weighed. The gas can splashed around the lawn, too heavy to pour consistently; a playful dance that almost distracted Marty from the darkness of his endeavor. He continued to traipse around the lawn until he had spilled enough to raise the can up in his arms. He poured it over Rocky's contorted form, uncertain if the suspended body was unconscious or unalive. He walked a careful trail around the lawn, keeping a safe distance from Carl, who still flickered orange every now and again. Finally, he returned to confront his bully.

Josh had collapsed, trying, and failing to release either leg from its trap. He still sang a warning, but it was winded now; a staccato trill. He coughed and found a new song as Marty splashed gasoline over the open wound in the bear trap, more across his prone form.

"Please, Marty," It was the pathetic howl of a trapped animal. Josh wasn't even present enough to attempt an apology. "Please don't do this."

Marty paused momentarily, regarding the pathetic remains of his bully. He considered their past encounters as he met wild, desperate eyes.

"Did begging ever work for me?"

Marty splashed gas around the area in a wide arc, finally tossing the can and whatever remained in Carl's direction. The red plastic jug bounced, liquid splashing harmlessly until it found enough flicker to ignite.

Marty dashed across the lawn, dodging wet patches that would soon catch, as well as other traps that his victims hadn't found. Not bothering to look back, he ran down the street toward home, hoping the fire was big enough to cover his tracks.

***

Marty thought he finally heard sirens as he climbed on top of the central air unit outside his bedroom window. He wondered what people would think – what they might say – when they started to pick apart the scene. He felt a little bad for whoever lived there; hopefully they wouldn't get in too much trouble.

He shook his head, clearing the fog of guilt as he quietly pushed the window open and slipped inside. Josh had caught him more than once on that block, and it was obvious that no one was home. Maybe if they were, things would have gone differently.

Marty closed the window gently and tugged his clothes off, leaving them lying in a trail across his floor. They were clingy; heavy with sweat. It had been a busy night.

His head hit the pillow and he wrinkled his nose. The acrid smell of things burned had collected in his hair. Marty sneezed and rubbed his nose into his pillow. He shuffled on the mattress, pressing his cheek deep into the down stuffing. He was already starting to drift off.

Tomorrow, the rumors would be all over school. How many of them would get close to the truth? He couldn't help but be curious. The counselor would pull him into their office at some point. It was sure to be a soft interrogation. Marty would assume his usual quiet demeanor and answer any questions pointed at him. It was highly unlikely that anyone would pick him as the culprit, but time would tell.

Tonight, he drew a deep, calm breath, exhaling slowly; he felt the weight of a job well done settling into his muscles and relaxed into a peaceful slumber.

Film to Digital

Jenifer Lynn

Clara peered through the viewfinder of her Pentax K1000 and slowly turned the focus ring until the split image in the circle aligned. The shutter click broke the pre-dawn silence of the graveyard. Pale gold streaks of sunrise had just started creeping through the moats of autumn fog that settled between the tombstones.

Felton Cemetery had been established in the mid 18th century as a small family cemetery on a rural farmstead. It grew as the town grew, adding family plots in sections to the west, then the south. In the 60's the township purchased what was left of the old farmstead, replacing it with a small chapel and expanding the cemetery to the east and south. The expansion eventually created a barrier of new, more modern headstones between civilization and the oldest graves. The original Felton family plots were all but overgrown, nestled against a thick grove of 200 year old pines.

It was at these oldest graves that Clara now stood, adjusting her camera settings. She had discovered the headstones during a camera-laden walk two weeks previous.

The sight of them, five uniquely carved stones covered by moss and vines, had enchanted her. The photos she had taken with her digital camera hadn't done them justice, however, so she decided to wait for a decently spooky atmosphere to come back with her film camera.

The unseasonably warm October weather had finally broken with a cool rain and dipping temperatures late the night before, guaranteeing the perfect morning mist. Leaves heavy with rain gathered around the old tombstones and stuck to her boots as she repositioned the tripod, focusing on a stone at the end of the row. They were all difficult to read, but after studying the images from her digital camera, she had deciphered four of the five. Mildred and Francis Felton were likely the matriarch and patriarch of the original Felton family, living long lives until they passed away in their 80s near the turn of the century, just a few months apart.

The other two were obviously their children. Carvings of angel's wings and the words "Beloved Daughter" were etched above their names. Milli and Christine, aged 7 years, died the same day in 1765. Was it an accident, an illness? So many things could have stolen those little ones away from their family during that time. She had tried searching the internet, but was unable to find anything solid about the family and their fate.

The fifth stone, the one she focused on now, had been unreadable, though a carving of a snake, maybe a long bodied dragon, twisted along the top. The growth of the foliage between the looping body gave the illusion that the creature had twisted itself around the vines rather than the other way around. The shutter clicked again, startling something in the darkened forest beyond the stones. Hurried movement deep in the shadows and the crack of grounded sticks.

Clara shivered, keeping her gaze away from the forest, not wanting to see what might lurk there, focusing instead on the viewfinder until her film was depleted. She shook off the chill as she packed up, using her digital camera to snap a few more photos of the mysterious headstone in the hopes that one of them would help her see beneath the centuries to the name underneath.

***

That afternoon Clara stood in the dim red of her darkroom, jaw slack as she stared at the first photo of the undecipherable headstone. The mist had turned out perfect, adding a haze along the bottom of the print that almost seemed to swirl in the still image. The contrast between the darkened forest background, and the sun-streaked foreground was exactly what she had hoped for.

The young man sitting on the headstone, however, was a surprise.

His head was bent forward, dark waves obscuring his face. His loose-fitting shirt had seen better days, and his trousers were ragged. His feet, semi-obscured by the mist, were bare and muddy.

She shook her head, searching the Photography 101 textbooks logged in her brain for a feasible explanation. Double exposure, maybe? Something wrong with the film?

She moved on to the next print. And the next. And the next. She hung them together in a row, watching in wonder as the man's head changed position from one frame to the next, looking toward the stones of the little girls. By the last frame, his face was turned toward the camera.

He couldn't have been much older than Clara, early twenties at best. His face was clean, handsome. His eyes were bright, showing as the palest gray on the black and white print. His lips quirked into a secretive half-smile.

He was there. Really there, not a trick of the film. And he had been looking right at her.

Clara left the prints to hang, a fluttering in her stomach. She brushed off her mother's insistence on having lunch as she passed through the kitchen on the way to her bedroom. Her digital camera sat on her computer desk, memory card unread.

***

That evening she sat with her head in her hands, blinking at the computer screen. The prints were splayed out on her desk, the final one held in her hand to the side of the computer screen. He wasn't in any of the digital images. She had used the digital camera seconds after the last frame of film, and yet he was gone.

"Clara?" her mother opened her door, "Clara, I made pizza with little black olive spiders on it." She wiggled her fingers. "Spooooky pizza to celebrate the thinning of the veil between worlds," she added, her voice wavering for dramatic effect.

"Halloween is tomorrow, Mom," Clara sighed.

"Spooooooooooky pizza," her mother insisted.

Mentally spent, Clara turned off her computer monitor, hoping that food would somehow make the day make sense.

***

Felton Cemetery was lit with a pale glow, the moonlight refracting through the mists that covered the ground.

"Clara..." a whisper slid through the chilled air.

She passed the chapel that stood watch, leaves crunching under her bare feet on the path back to the old gravestones, following the voice. She found him there, sitting just like in her photograph. He looked up as she approached and stood, holding out his hand to her. The moonlight played strange on his pale, grayscale face, not working as normal light should, casting shadows in the wrong direction.

She took his hand, allowing him to pull her into an embrace. His shirt was itchy linen on her cheek, real and solid. His arms wrapped around her were warm, strong, and steady. That warmth spread through her body, chasing away the night's chill.

"Who are you?" she asked in a trembling, small voice.

His arms tightened around her. *"Come find me."*

***

Clara put a hand to her chest as she gasped for breath, sitting up in bed. Her room was silent and still, her heart thumping in her ears. The eerie blue light of her computer monitor filled the room and instinctively she turned to see the screen. The dragon atop the mysterious headstone stared out of the image with pale stone eyes.

Her dream lingered, the whispered words twisting through her consciousness.

Come find me, Clara.

***

"At least the rain stopped," Clara's mother was saying. "Kids'll catch a cold if they trick or treat in the rain."

"That's not how it works, Mom," Clara responded, pulling a box of slides from the bottom of a gray tub. "You're sure it was in this bin?"

Her mother put a finger to her lips. "Hmmm, maybe it was that one." She nodded to a second gray storage bin two shelves higher.

Clara stifled her sigh and stood, pulling the heavy bin down and failing to set it gently onto the concrete basement floor. An old projector nested in the center inhibited the use of a lid, and Clara brushed away ten years of spider webs before she found what she was looking for.

"I'm sure the film is no good," her mother said. "But I think the art supply store still carries it. But it's expensive. Do you need money?"

Clara brushed dust off the old Polaroid and smiled. "Yes, please."

***

It was almost dark by the time Clara made it back to Felton Cemetery. Her mother had made her take the first shift passing out candy for the trick or treaters, reminding her that she had shelled out $40 for polaroid film earlier in the day. The woods beyond the gravestones were hidden in shadow, but the stones themselves were lit by the last rays of the setting sun.

Clara loaded the pack of film, 10 exposures, and immediately took a photo of the mysterious headstone. The flash went off automatically, startling her. She pulled the undeveloped image from the front of the camera and put it gently in the pocket of her jacket as she set up the tripod. Next she attached a self-timer her mother had created years ago for family pictures, a rudimentary spring and clamp glued to a small kitchen timer that would take a photo every 15 seconds once the dial was turned.

When she was done, she pulled the first photo from her pocket and held it up to the last light of sunset so she could see. Her heart hammered against her ribcage.

He was there. Turned toward her, hand outstretched.

She took a deep breath, putting the photo back into her pocket. "Okay," she whispered to herself. "Here we go."

She turned the dial on the timer, and stepped forward. One step, then another, hand outstretched.

The flash went off, blinding her temporarily, and then she felt him. His hand sliding into hers. She gasped despite herself, willing her eyes to adjust in the darkness. There was nothing there, but she felt him pull her forward. Wet toilet paper clung to the low branches above the Felton Cemetery gate.

Another bright flash and she closed her eyes, feeling the itchy linen of his shirt against her cheek. The warmth from her dream flooded through her as she felt his arms wrap around her.

"Who are you?" she asked.

Another bright flash shone bright red against her closed eyelids and she saw him in her mind's eye, bending down to whisper in her ear. "Thank you." She could hear his voice clear and real. "Thank you for finding me, Clara."

She heard movement in the woods beyond the stones, and opened her eyes, looking through the invisible boy that held her and into the darkness. Another flash and she squeezed her eyes shut again, the after images of two long-limbed figures, low, crawling on the forest floor, danced behind her eyelids.

"Thank you," the young man said again, "because we've been so, so very hungry."

Clara felt a sharp pain in her shoulder and she opened her mouth to scream, but the warmth that surrounded her muted the sound. Another flash and she felt a sharp pain in her leg under the knee. And another in the arm that struggled against the invisible force that held her.

Another flash, and her muted screams were choked and silence fell once again in the graveyard.

***

Terry frowned, pulling the rake from the back of his truck and reached up, scraping against the bark, pulling up tiny pieces of the tissue. He muttered to himself, holding his aching back as he lowered the rake. "Stupid kids. Stupid Halloween." He tossed the rake back into the truck. "Stupid rake. Stupid back."

He climbed into the cab of his truck and started past the chapel and into the cemetery. There was always something, and even worse on Halloween. From pranks to illicit activities, Terry had to handle it all. That's what the township paid him for, and that's what he would do.

"Stupid Halloween," he grumbled again, hopping out of his truck on the west side of the cemetery to peel melted candle wax off the low, wide Trelawny Family headstone.

An hour later he had found a discarded shoe and a ladies undergarment on the east end, and cleaned new graffiti off the Grant mausoleum. The back of the cemetery with the oldest headstones loomed in his mind, and he managed to find another half hour's worth of chores to do before he made it back there.

He rarely came all the way back here, mostly because no one else did, so he could get away with it. The woods were dark, despite the bright noon sun. He squinted at the stones, frowning. "What the hell...?"

Grudgingly, he got out of the cab of his truck and approached the graves. An old Polaroid camera stood on a tripod about ten feet from the headstones. Polaroid images were haphazardly thrown to the ground, face down, in front of the tripod. He bent over to collect the images, wincing at the pain in his lower back.

The first image was blurry, but the second was of a young couple in what seemed to be a passionate embrace. He raised his eyebrows and flipped to the next image. Not much had changed, except there were two figures in the woods behind the couple now, barely visible in the shadows. In the next image, the figures were clearer, two gaunt young girls crawled on all fours, eyes sunken back into their skulls, bony arms stretching forward to pull themselves onto the headstones. The young man had lifted his head, staring back at the camera with bright, glowing amber eyes.

The man's head bent again into the woman's shoulder, blood oozed from an unseen wound, staining her shirt. One of the young girls had wrapped skeletal arms tight around her leg, long sharp teeth sinking into her flesh.

In the next image, the woman was on the ground, the man dragging her by the arm toward the woods. The two children clung to her, teeth and claws holding fast while their legs dragged lifelessly behind them.

There wasn't anything of note in the last two images. All of the figures had disappeared from view leaving a peaceful scene of the gravestones at night. Terry looked up and into the woods, bushy white eyebrows drawn together. After a long moment he sighed, throwing the pictures, camera, and tripod into the back of his truck.

The truck's engine broke the eerie silence, and Terry shook his head, throwing one last glance at the woods.

"Stupid kids," he grumbled. "Stupid Halloween."

TESOUT ROAD

Relics

Jess Boldt

A worn green street sign creaked and shook in the autumn wind, shaking particles of rust from the dutiful bolts that had held it atop the steel post for an endless procession of seasons. The specks of rust were pushed forward by a second gust of wind, joining them in a swirling mass of dust and dead leaves, leaving the sign post behind, the post that marked Tesout Road. The mass of debris accumulated as it went towards the old town center. Each time it touched ground, another push of wind would lift it back up, bigger, more complex, as it picked up hitchhiking gum wrappers, discarded cigarette butts, and forgotten bits of discard and refuse.

This cloud of dust and refuse danced past the trestle bridge which stood watch over a dark river, past the hill where small homes and shops gave way to a boulevard of buildings, mostly brick, all lit up from the inside like hearths, slowly warming the inhabitants and patrons of the various establishments. The sidewalks were full of people trying their best to not look like people. A makeshift parade of goblins, witches, cloaked vampires, and every other imaginable-wicked now made fun creatures that the citizens of the old town could conjure.

The collection of clutter had reached such a mass that the wind seemed to become fatigued, perhaps broken by the surrounding buildings, and finally, with one final gust, scattered the debris of leaves, dust, and rust on the sidewalk in front of a warmly lit wood and glass door. Above that door, painted in white letters read, "Gene's Arcade and Pizzeria."

The inside of Gene's Arcade and Pizzeria, at least the Pizzeria side, was filled with costumed patrons. The arcade side had long stood dormant with silent machines that once provided colorful electronic entertainment to the kids of a bygone era. The patrons of the pizzeria were full of spirit and cheer inside the establishment. Some crammed into the large wooden booths that hugged the walls around the perimeter. Each one filled with coveted pitchers of beer and pizza pies raised high on metal bases. Others were gathered around the oak bar that was the centerpiece of the room. The large horseshoe bar jutted out from the kitchen in the back, its lacquered surface hosting a rotation of pint glasses, shot glasses, bottles, and cans.

Behind the bar, a man worked feverishly to make sure no patron knew a dry glass or empty bottle. He darted from one customer to another with a precision and concentration that made his task look easy to the patrons. Someone would call out, "Tommy, another round!" or

"Tom, My Boy, a drink for my friend!" and he would brush his brown hair back from his eyes, smile, and point for confirmation as if it was second nature. His stride would only stop when the waitress, Erica, would come up to the service area with a new order. Her curly red hair, partially hidden by a green witches hat she wore, bounced around her head as she went from one station to the next. Each time she had come to the bar with a slip, she was all Tommy saw, and he was all she saw. And so, for a moment, the pace and rhythm of service slowed, though there was never a complaint.

As the night wore on, the crowd dissipated, onto other Halloween night adventures, or perhaps home to hand out candy to the most hardy of trick-or-treaters, or clean up toilet paper from trees or other such reminders of mischief typical of this night. It was at this transition, an older man with grey hair walked in. A scar ran across his face, broken by the eye-patch he wore. A brown trench coat hung around his aging, yet robust frame. He looked around the pizzeria until he saw a woman with shoulder length blonde hair sitting at the booth. Across from her sat a small girl with auburn hair, she was dressed as a black cat, complete with tail and ears.

The older man smiled and waved, and as if that wave held a frequency only audible to little girls masquerading as felines, the girl turned around. Her expression grew bright as she jumped from her sitting position. "Grandpa!" she yelled as she sprung down from the seat and pounced on the floor. She dashed into his open arms, her fabric tail swinging as he picked her up. After a tight embrace, he put the girl down. "How's Halloween treating you, Sara?"

"Great," she exclaimed. "I got so much candy. Well, I could have gotten more but mom said we should get some dinner," Sara stated, as she straightened her cat ear headband.

"You have enough candy to last until next year," the blonde woman said, putting her hand on Sara's back. "How are you doing, Dad?"

"I'm good, Julie," he said as he looked around the pizzeria. "I'm glad to see the old place is doing well. Although, I can't say I like seeing the arcade become a storage room," he said, pointing to a closed-off and darkened section near the front of the building.

"It won't be for long. Erica and I are turning it into extra dining space, we'll have it filled in no time," said Tommy who had come from the bar.

The man turned around and met Tommy's smile then shook his hand. "I suppose it's a good move, but back then, that place was really something," the old man said.

"It wasn't an easy decision, Gene, but Julie approved the idea. It's just with this place so busy and now that kids play video games at home, well, it just kind of got abandoned," Tommy said.

Gene smiled and nodded. "I put you in charge of running the place, and I can't see any reason to regret that decision, as long as Julie approves, of course, but does this mean that you'll be changing the name? You can't really go around calling it an arcade and pizzeria if there isn't any arcade."

"Actually, Dad, I said we should keep it. It has a historical quality to it. Besides, we'll leave a few machines running once renovations are complete, so technically it'll still be accurate," Julie said before guiding Sara back to her.

"Well, anyway, you've done a terrific job managing the place. You and Erica both," Gene stated within earshot of Erica who was taking an order from a group of youths, three boys; one dressed as a mummy, another a skeleton, and monster accompanied by one girl dressed as a witch. They were rolling a small pumpkin back and forth between each other while listing off their orders. She turned, waved, and smiled warmly at Gene.

Gene sat next to Sara who was already working on a new slice of cheese and mushroom. Julie smiled at him and reached out her hand to cup over his. "How are things back at the house? I know you're capable of the upkeep but it can't be easy with," she drew in a quick breath, "with mom gone."

Gene's expression soured for a moment then warmed.

"Just like I told you last week, and the week before, I'm fine. It's a solid house, always has been. Besides, fixing a leak or scraping some paint here and there keeps me busy." He smiled and let out a huff. "I swear it's like you think I'm some withered piece of fruit that's just about ready to fall from the limb."

"It's not that. I just, well, I don't know..." Julie trailed off. "I've just been thinking about your home. Not where you live, but where you came from. You've talked about your sister so many times. Your hometown, your family. I know that was so long ago, but haven't you ever wanted to go back, visit? I know you aren't frail, just the opposite. I just don't want to see you miss your opportunity. I know the road is..."

Gene removed his hand from under hers and placed it on top. "The past is the past, and I've made quite a life here. One that I'm proud of. It's a fine town, but more importantly, I have you and Sara," he said with a smile as he tussled Sara's hair with his free hand. She returned the affection by hissing like a cat before grabbing another slice.

"I just see that look in your eye sometimes. I know you're thinking about that road."

"That doesn't mean I want to go back. The two of you are the most important things in my life, and even seeing my home again can't compare to that."

Sara tugged at her grandfather's coat. "Can I check out

the old game room?"

Gene smiled at the young girl then glanced over at her mother.

"Just be careful, it's pretty dark in there and there's plenty to trip on," Julie responded.

Gene reached inside his coat and pulled out a handful of coins. He dropped them into Sara's open hands. "I told them to keep the frog game and that other one you like plugged in."

Without further instruction, Sara climbed over her grandfather, walked past the patrons and into the dark room. A moment later, the dark entrance to the room was illuminated by flashing blues, reds, and greens.

Julie took in a deep breath and stared into her father's remaining eye. "The truth is, I know why you stick around. I know how much you love us, of course I do. Sara knows it too. But there's something else, another reason you haven't even tried to see if getting home was possible."

Gene's expression grew dark and slow. "Oh?"

"And I have no doubt you would come back after seeing what's left of home. The real reason is that you still think you have to protect us. Not just Sara and I, but this entire town. You spent years keeping this town safe from what came out of those woods. But this town has been safe since," Julie closed her eyes as she put her palm to her cheek. "...since we almost lost everything," she finished.

Gene stared at Julie for a long moment. "That was a long time ago. Leave the old memories in the past."

Julie looked up, her expression stone. "Have you let go? Mom told me about the nights she would wake up in an empty bed only to fall asleep and see you in the morning smelling of those woods. You haven't stopped looking, have you, Dad?"

"I, uh, I tried. After everything that happened, the attacks, deaths, the... Christ, this town never even realized the dangers, and after everything, they've just forgotten. Sure, they always ignored the witches, monsters, and everything else that came from those damn woods, but just to forget about what happened those years ago when everything came to a head and this town burned..." Gene shook his head slowly. "Well, someone has to keep watch. Those who remember, who remember the losses..." Gene trailed off, his stare now off into the distance.

"Dad, it's been years since anything came out of those woods. Hell, people are living near them now and the worst thing that you hear about from there is some drunkard beating on his neighbor's car with a nine iron."

Gene raised his eyebrow in an inquisitive gesture.

"It was something I read in the paper. What I'm trying to say is that maybe those that forgot everything are the lucky ones. They don't remember a town where monsters came lurking out of the shadows to take people at night, where witches roamed abandoned houses to seduce the youth, where we had to watch our friends fight and die," she stopped, her eyes moved around the room as if attempting to avoid something invisible but always present. She took a breath and re-focused on her father.

"I went out because I can't be sure that things won't start over, that those woods won't reawaken and we won't be ready," Gene said as he rubbed his hand through his thick gray hair. He frowned, lines earned by his age grew around his face. "And I guess, a small part of me was hoping to find something. Maybe not the monsters, or a real threat, but something that I could prove myself on. Something more than a leaky faucet, or squeaky hinge. I suppose that doesn't make much sense to you."

Julie's eyes burned through her father for a moment. Lines of worry, and a bit of anger, drew upon her face. She began to open her mouth, but Gene raised a hand to interject.

"I haven't been going as often since your mom passed. A couple of times, but that was months ago. Still doesn't make me any less of a fool," he said, lowering his head from her stare.

"You aren't a fool, and those of us who remember know best the kind of man you are. But let the past be the past, just as you keep telling us. This town doesn't need vigilance, it needs to move forward. So do you. I don't know if that means puttering around the house and fixing stuff up or maybe taking that trip that's been on your mind for far too long."

The two sat there for a while, barely talking at first until a few quips grew into small talk which grew into conversations. Not of cursed woods, witches, or a town with no memory, but memories kept together, from the brief recollections to the large moments that weaved through their lives. This continued until Sara, the black cat, had come back to the table and reached over for a now cold slice of pizza. Julie forced herself out of the fog of memories and smiled.

"I guess we should be getting home. I told Dan we would stop by for trick-or-treats," she said as she stood up.

Gene nodded. "The place seems to be clearing out. I guess it's time for me to get home as well."

Gene stood up and hugged Sara, then hugged Julie. "Happy Halloween," he said.

"Haphhy Hurerween," said the young girl, still chewing on crust.

"Happy Halloween, Dad," said Julie as she took Sara by the hand.

The two of them walked out into the breezy autumn night. Gene waited until he couldn't see them anymore and took a look around the place. He could almost hear the sounds of the old arcade, full of the local youth yelling over the electronic sounds. He was lost to that time, that memory that played out like a thousand memories layered on top of each other and created a warm, constant hum.

"Want a drink before we shut down, Gene?"

Gene snapped himself out of the haze of nostalgia and turned around to see Tommy standing behind the bar. The man was wiping down the surface with an old rag that had, maybe, once been white.

"Damnit, Tommy, you have to use a clean rag. You're..." Gene stopped, his face reddened. "Sorry, I went into my old boss mode. A drink? No, stuff keeps me up."

Tommy smiled and threw the old rag behind the bar. "Erica gets on me about the rags all the time. Bad habit, I guess."

"Don't think anything of it. You've done this place well. Although, I have to say, Erica does a great job, but don't you think you should bring on some more servers?

Tommy smiled at Gene and shook his head. "Trust me, I have begged her to let me split her shifts with a new person. She won't hear of it," he frowned then continued in a low voice. "She's so much better than she was, but still, I think work keeps her busy enough not to think of things."

Gene turned around and watched Erica bus one of the last remaining tables. He nodded then turned back to Tommy. "I understand that. Keeping busy is often the best medicine. Well, I guess I'll get out of your hair and let you close up. Keep up the good work."

"Gene, uh, just wanted to let you know, it's probably nothing, just some kids or something. But there's been talk about people seeing shadows out in the woods, near Tesout. I've been meaning to check it out, but well, business being so, well busy..."

Gene's eye widened for a moment, then he laughed. "Don't worry about it. Like you said, kids. Probably over the moon they found a spot to drink and carry on. It was bound to happen sooner or later. If anything else starts to happen, let me know. But for now, just enjoy your success."

Gene walked up to the bar and pounded it with his sturdy fist. He smiled at Tommy and then turned around while raising a hand 'goodbye' to Erica who was now bussing dishes back to the kitchen. He proceeded to walk out into the night. Up the road he watched the porch lights flicker off like fireflies in the neighborhoods. He stretched, taking in the cool air and began walking towards them.

Gene made it a few steps past the downtown district when he stopped. He stood there for a while, as a group of cloistered people in costume parted to avoid him, only to reconvene after passing. He turned around and walked away from town, past the building with his name on it. He walked past the shops and small houses until he came into view of the trestle overlooking the river. He made his way down and walked adjacent to the banks of the river until he came to a street sign, now silent atop its steel post. The houses on the street had mostly darkened porches, except for a few hosting last minute trick-or-treaters. Older kids mostly, probably waiting out the last light to start some traditional mischief.

He walked down the road, stopping at one house in particular, it was dark, the shadows concealing years of neglect barely made visible by the orange street light that hummed overhead. He walked past the abandoned house, its peeling paint, broken windows, and warped wood, towards the thicket of wood and vegetation that stood silent past the backyard.

The forest ahead of him was dark and silent, thick with overgrowth of brambles, nettles, fallen trees and blackberry bushes. Gene leaned over and picked up a thick limb covered in chipping bark and green moss. Stepping forward, he lifted a branch with the hefty limb, revealing a well worn path in the darkness. With his free arm, he held the branches and thorns that reached out for him, only to sting fabric. He dropped the limb where he picked it up, entering the woods, allowing its guardians of nettles and brush to continue their watch after he passed.

Gene continued down the path, as much as it was, the canopy overhead selfish to the little moonlight it would allow. Each step Gene made was confident, not lacking pace or precision. He had walked these woods for decades now, maybe longer than that. Each crunch of vegetation or kicked rock was familiar to him, even though the individual plants would change and shift, the path remained the same.

He had walked for less than a half hour when the familiarity was broken by a single snap of a branch. He froze, not out of fear, but rather an anticipation he hadn't felt in some time. An electric surge that brought the memory of years past back, through every cell and circuit the energy traveled. Another snap, a limb pushed. Gene breathed in the air, and steeled himself, holding the thrill of this electricity.

There, he could hear the footsteps dart from a hesitant step to a dead run. A dark figure burst from vegetation, jetting out from the figure was a flash of silver. Gene spun and reached his arm out to grab the figure by its arms. 'Damn, too slow,' he thought as the shock of the slice grazed his hand up to his arm. His hands found their purchase on the black cloak of the figure despite the miscalculation. He pulled the figure towards him in a burst and rammed his forehead into the void of the dark robe, guessing where the face would be. There was a blunt audible thud as the figure let out a wail of pain as the sound of the bright knife dropped to the ground below. Gene froze. 'The monsters never cried out,' he thought. Wasting no time, he shoved the figure hard against a tree, feeling its resistance crumple upon impact. He dropped the figure to the ground and leaned down to pick up the dropped silver knife.

Gene pulled out a small flashlight and showed it at the whimpering figure. "Who are you?" Gene demanded as he held the moonlit weapon, blood from his wound running down the blade. The figure slowly reached up to its cowl, groaning in pain. In the artificial light, the figure revealed himself. A young, scrawny man with thick matted hair that clung to the side of his face, now fresh with blood flowing from the wound on his forehead.

The man's patchy facial hair trembled as he began to speak with effort. "Y-you, you bastard. Wait until she hears. The witch h-hears all. This is her d-domain and soon all of..."

Gene moved the flashlight closer to the man's head. After a brief examination, his expression narrowed. "Nicky. I remember you. Just a punk kid who stole beer then moved on to bigger things, bigger but dumber things." Gene gestured to the woods around him. "So this is what has become of you? An imitation of a shadow, jumping out of the dark, pretending to be," Gene gripped the silver knife. "Pretending to be just a shadow that should be forgotten."

The man scowled and made a jerk forward only to have his pain crash him back to the base of the tree. "I'm the same as what used to haunt these woods. My eyes may be different, but I'm the same. I'm not the loser you remember. And she's just as powerful as anything that has made this place their home. She is going to give me such power, just wait, JUST YOU WAIT!" he finished in a scream, tears welling up in his eyes.

"The same," Gene responded with a slight laugh. "Boy, you wouldn't have lasted twenty seconds with one of them. You can barely wield their weapons."

'Jesus,' he thought, 'how long would I have lasted if this man was really one of them? He even drew some blood. I wouldn't have even heard a real one coming.'

The man groaned. "Just wait until she finds you, she won't stand for this. I can't be treated this way, not ever aga..." Nicky choked, his voice trailed off into a slow sob.

Gene turned off his flashlight, leaving Nicky in the darkness. The pain of his arm flooded his brain. He grimaced, then tore off a piece of cloth from his sleeve. He bandaged himself the best he could and continued walking. Leaving the sounds of wet sobbing behind him.

He moved through thicket and wood, each step a memory. Memories that shouldn't be pleasant, yet he found them comforting. 'What's wrong with me?' he asked himself as he recollected a dozen battles, hundreds of close calls, faces that were no longer here to share stories. Then out of the fog of memory he saw new faces. There was Julie who dressed as a fairy going house to house, begging for candy on a Halloween night, much like this. He remembered worrying for her the moment she got out of his sight, even for a moment. He then thought of Sara, and the realization that her Halloweens would be much different. The realization that the only monster would be store-bought or mother-sewn. That realization washed over his body, and while it wasn't the intensity of the electric exhilaration he experienced earlier, it was, in many ways, the most profound feeling he had ever experienced.

'You old fool,' he thought to himself.

As he walked, he noticed a white light in the near distance. He paused and looked around, trying to place himself. Up ahead should be the clearing. There's an old 76 station up there. A graveyard of memories that no longer gave up the comfort of nostalgia. He walked forward, almost forcing himself as the trees and brush gave way to a small clearing that hosted the ruins of an old filling station. Concrete blocks created a perimeter around what used to be the building. As he walked, orange plastic from an old display crushed beneath his feet. He brought the silver weapon out and held it tight in his good hand that, despite his efforts, trembled.

At first there was nothing under the unfettered light of the moon. But then motion, the figure of a woman emerged from the center of the ruins, her face young, framed by black hair. A tattered black dress flowed around her body, up to her neck. She glared directly at Gene, a broken smile illuminated by the white light from a service light still connected to the remains of a wall from which it was mounted. The woman hissed, "You aren't Nicky. No, you... what are you doing in my woods?"

Gene stood still as the woman approached. She walked with a noticeable limp over the broken orange plastic and rubble. "Do you think I'm just another witch? I'm much more than that." She hissed then stopped. Her eyes grew wide as she saw the silver knife in his hands. "You aren't welcome here. Go. Go before I," the woman's speech broke. "What have you done with Nicky?"

Gene took a step back and stared at the woman then he took a deep breath in. "So, I guess they were right, there isn't any real danger left in these woods. Just a bunch of fools who can't let go. Fine company we make."

The woman drew back, nearly tripping over the remnants of a cement block covered in growth. "You come to my home and tell me I am no danger. I have made deals with the old powers, I have been granted youth again. I am nothing to sneer at, Gene," she said, steadying herself. She then coughed, a wretched, deep cough. Gene could see the youthful glow of skin decay as years of lines and wrinkles and gravity took over, showing her to be an old woman, one that Gene recognized. A woman, not unlike Nicky, who sought to join with the old magic, the forgotten magic of the woods. Someone willing to sacrifice deeply just for the security of freezing themselves in a moment rather than face the relentless progression of time. She breathed in two deep panicked breaths, and her youthful facade returned.

"You are no witch. You're a relic from a different time in this town, not unlike me. Where we differ is that these woods whispered false promises to you, and you answered. I know you, May. Just a parasite that is living off the dust of whatever magic, or whatever it was, that used to seep from these grounds and linger in the air. You barely have enough of that to keep yourself in mask. Was it worth it?" Gene asked solemnly as he recalled the headlines of her daughter's mysterious murder. Murder? No, it was a sacrifice.

"I gave them blood. I made the deal long ago, and I can't be denied. I.." May went into another coughing fit, her youth fading into the dark recess of age again. "I.. I am supposed to live forever. I will. I will find a way. Then I will give you the death you seek in these woods."

Gene tossed the silver knife into the void of the darkness. "These may have been foolish years, but they've been good years. Something you've sold away for nothing more than a cosmetic magic trick. Killing you would be a mercy you don't deserve. The only dangers you possess are the memories that will surely eat away at you until the end. That is if you have any soul left in that fake body of yours," he said, as he walked past the rubble and the old woman grasping for breath.

"You can't leave me here, thinking you've won. I'm

powerful, I'm young, I will always be young," she wailed, desperate for scarce air.

Gene ignored the woman and walked into the forest in front of him. Her gasping faded as he walked back over more familiar ground. Each step put distance between him and May, and Nicky, and perhaps a bit of himself. The silence of the forest broke with the sound of owl calls, creatures hunting and hiding, insects jumping in the cool autumn night. The stillness moved into motion with every step until the forest broke and parted to a concrete road. He stopped and planted his feet steady on the road. Everything led him to the one place he wasn't planning on visiting. He drew his coat around himself, now noticing the chill of the night. He looked to his right, a road that would lead back into town. Then he looked to his left, the same road but a path he had not been on for a long time. The path Julie encouraged him to take. He looked right again. Past the trees, far in the distance, he could see the glow of the town peeking above the canopy. He took one last look to the left and nodded. "Maybe someday, but not tonight," he said to himself.

He walked down the road, towards town, each step lighter despite the lateness of the hour. After some time he found himself back amongst the buildings and streets of the town. The quietness of the night still echoed the memories of Halloween. Discarded candy wrappers, trees with toilet paper hanging from the branches, paper monsters and witches clinging to store-front windows, and the pumpkins whose features were now dark, their candles burnt out.

As fatigue and a new relief overtook Gene, he felt an encouraging gust of wind push against his back. He went onward, watching as the wind picked up some of those candy wrappers, along with the debris of dust, rust, and dead leaves. He watched as the wind struggled then gained speed, sending them off to somewhere unknown, but always forward.

I Know a Place

Andy Lockwood

Costumed figures large and small raced along the streets, calling to one another through the smoky night air. The evening was full of promise: the scent of confections, the crinkle of candy wrappers, and the glimmer of dollar store toys ghosted along behind every child as they moved from house to house. To the casual observer, it seemed nothing so different from watching schools of piranha as water levels recede. They swarmed food sources, churning and devouring until nothing was left but another closed and darkened doorway.

Crowds flocked to The Heights at Halloween: lavish lawns, expensive holiday displays, and full-size candy bars. The dream of Heights-life brought half the city to the winding streets of the extravagant locality. Even kids who might have aged out of trick-or-treating in other neighborhoods were not turned away here. It was four square blocks of sodium-lit American Dream.

Tony, Elle, and Janey watched the dream in action from across the street. To them, it was more of a nightmare each passing year: desperate, hungry masses; a meat grinder made of people. They skirted the throngs of masked envy, avoiding The Heights and its huddled masses altogether. Less than fifty feet from The Heights, nestled in the shadow of the overpriced hilltop, rested the Woodfield neighborhood. When they were done watching the chaos in The Heights, the trio turned and followed the sidewalk into the smaller, more modest neighborhood.

Woodfield was a haven for older folks on this end of town. The winding streets kept speeds low and discouraged commuters from cutting through. There was also the promise of as much candy as The Heights, with fewer trick-or-treaters.

At least, that's what Mrs. Westerberg promised Elle earlier in the week. Elle had seen her struggling with a scarecrow at the end of her walkway. Elle didn't need to be asked; she stopped, holding the wooden post in place while the old woman affixed it with wire to the metal lamp light.

"How fortunate that you were walking down the street when I needed assistance," yellow teeth smiled up at Elle in a display of warmth. "Let me show my appreciation."

"No, really, that's not –" Elle began, but wrinkled fingers had already grasped her wrist, pulling her along to the house. She left Elle on the porch as she rummaged inside the door. A moment later, she re-emerged, offering a choice of candy bars.

"Please, take one... or two." She peered at Elle over her glasses. "It can be our secret."

"Wow, you sure like candy!"

"Oh, these aren't for me. Though, I'm not sure why I even bother." She took a deep breath, looking wistfully up the block at the rising hills across the boulevard. "No one trick-or-treats around here anymore. Last year, I gave three to any child who stopped by. I was still left with so many."

Three? Elle swallowed; it seemed too good to be true.

"I still like to see the costumes and hear the children. It reminds me of when I was young."

Elle smiled. "I didn't know you were so into Halloween."

"I'll let you in on a secret," Mrs. Westerberg smiled, leaning in conspiratorially. "Growing old doesn't mean you have to grow up."

They shared a laugh, then Mrs. Westerberg shooed Elle with a wave.

"Most of the neighborhood gives out as much candy as The Heights, but no one wants to cross the street to find out."

***

It didn't take much convincing to get Tony and Janey to trick-or-treat in a new area – especially with the looming promise of more candy than they could stomach. They all agreed The Heights were problematic: too many kids, too much pushing. It was fun when they were younger, but the brick-laid streets of the stately neighborhood were overrun now. The candy supply was simply not meeting demand.

They stopped at the first house on the street, approaching the low stoop and its friendly jack-o-lanterns. Tony fumbled with his candy bucket, almost dropping it yet again as he overcorrected his balance under the ever-shifting weight of the comically oversized gecko head strapped to his own.

"This is the last time I let my mom pick out my costume." He stomped his feet, both his tail and googly eyes bouncing wildly.

"Oh stop – it's a really good costume," the cobbled-together witch grumbled. Janey gestured at her librarian glasses, schoolgirl skirt, scientist's lab coat, wizard hat, and fairy wand. "I don't think there's a single fantasy world where I wouldn't be ridiculed for this outfit."

Elle leaned into Janey, gently squeezing her close. "Hey – your mom tried."

Both the gecko and witch looked sheepishly at Elle, acknowledging her point. No one talked about what Elle's mom did to keep a roof over their heads – at least not in front of Elle. Plenty of kids at school whispered, but the truth was Elle didn't know enough to refute the rumors. She didn't know any better than they did, though the facts did lean heavily in their favor. Her mom slept all day and was gone all night. Elle didn't trouble her mom if she could help it; instead choosing to work around the neighborhood for fun money. In the evening, her mom was the most pleasant – cheerful, even – as she tried to catch up with Elle's day. She was also anxious and sometimes distracted. In the morning, she was either angry or loopy; it was anybody's guess which. It was easier to be out of the way in the summer, but as the weather turned cool, her mom seemed to have less work and more time to be angry.

Tony and Janey both smiled at her. She'd put together a pretty good magician costume. The tux looked authentic, complete with collapsible top hat. She even learned a couple of tricks in case someone asked. The wand was the real deal – and the hardest trick to master. With a flick of her wrist, it transformed into a bouquet; another flick did the reverse – most of the time. With a stuffed rabbit and a fake dove, she was all set to amaze.

"Trick or treat!"

The old woman looked surprised as she opened the door. She adjusted her glasses and smiled at Elle. "You came back! Well, just look at you three! My stars!" She turned back to the hallway, rummaging around until she produced an armful of candy bars. They could feel the weight of their first stop hit the bottom of their treat bags.

"Be sure to swing by before you finish up. I'm sure I'll have a few left at the end of the night." They thanked her in unison, turning to rush back down the sidewalk. Tony shook his bucket before swinging it over his head.

"Everything is going to hurt tomorrow. My arms, my stomach, my teeth... It's going to be awesome."

"Maybe you could pace yourself a little."

"Maybe you could shut up."

They laughed down the first block. Not every porch was lit, but when they were, each stop was a trove of goodies. Full-size candy bars, five-dollar bills, and toys; it was baffling that more kids weren't running around the neighborhood. It should have been more popular than The Heights.

"Why isn't it?" Janey finally asked. They had finished

the first full street and already, shoulders ached and fingers strained.

"Does it matter?" Tony managed a handful of syllables around a mouthful of candy.

Janey stared at her shoes as she avoided cracks and concrete seams. "It's just weird. This isn't the kind of thing anyone would keep secret. If anyone knew, they'd bring their friends, right?"

They paused as a group, looking up and down the streets. Porches were lit sporadically throughout the neighborhood, jack-o-lanterns glowed from steps all over. Paper decorations clung to living room windows. It seemed idyllic. The only thing missing was the sound of other children. Any children at all.

Their nervous breathing was painfully obvious on the quiet street. No birds, dogs, or even kids to speak of. The neighborhood was eerily silent as if shunning the trio for their discovery.

"Maybe we should go," Elle spoke, jumping at how loud her whisper sounded.

"No way," Tony spat, shaking his treat bag. "Have you seen this haul? We're not even halfway through!"

Elle and Janey looked at each other, then back to him. They squinted at one another, struggling to see in the failing light. The streetlights never came on. Only the setting sun offered them light, and that was mostly shaded by the evergreen canopy.

"I'm not playing. This is starting to freak me out." Janey's whisper was sharp and insistent.

"Are you kidding? We have the neighborhood to ourselves and you want to leave."

"Tony! She's scared," Elle stomped her foot. "I am too."

He huffed. The silence lingered, stretching itself to ridiculous proportions in the dark.

"Fine."

"Thank you!" The girls cried together.

"One more house."

He scanned the crossroads, turning to the biggest and brightest of the houses. A long stretch of yard spread before the columned porch, a stone walkway splitting the sea of green. A small sign stuck out of the lawn, breaking up the perfectly manicured grounds.

KEEP OFF THE GRASS

They followed the sidewalk, stopping at the mouth of the walkway to the house. Large pavers were spaced at uneven distances from one another, seemingly further apart than the average adult's stride. Jack-o-lanterns secured the perimeter around the porch, glowering from steps and railings. At the top of the steps waited a tall figure in a hooded cloak.

The girls followed Tony up to the edge of the public sidewalk, where he paused. Even his costume features were painfully still while he hesitated. Elle prodded him with her wand.

"Well?"

Tony shot a look at Elle, then back to the stone path, before swallowing hard. The figure at the end of the walkway didn't seem so much like a person as it did a shadow occupying space. Even with the warm orange glow radiating from the front of the house, the shape was a black hole subsisting on candlelight.

Tony paused, then took a first step up the path to the house. His shoulders relaxed as his feet rested on the first of many stone steps along the footpath. Shuffling his feet, he got a running start and leapt to the next stone. Three deep, he turned to his friends.

"Well?" He parroted back at Elle. The googly eyes atop his head seemed to mock the girls of their own accord. Together, they followed Tony down the path; Hansel and Gretel and Gretel skipping deeper into the woods.

Finally reaching the porch, the shadow loomed. It was taller and darker than it had appeared from the sidewalk. It was perfectly still. They had no idea if it was a prop, a person, or something else.

"Um... Trick or treat?" Tony raised his candy bucket in a wavering hand.

"Trick. Or. Treat." The shadow replied in a sharp rattle. Its spine bent like a serpent to meet Tony at eye level. Two ancient hands struck out of the darkness holding a bag in its talon grasp. Tony yelped and stumbled back, bumping into Janey. She stuttered back before bracing them both against falling.

Whoever resided within the shroud was concealed. There was no way to know, no way to see. Delicate paper skin threatened to split over thin fingers as they held the bag tighter, shaking the contents.

"Trick. Or. Treat."

"Go on. This was your idea." Elle nudged Tony closer to the bag.

He breathed hard as he shuffled forward, looking into the darkness of the bag. It seemed both the bag and the hood were fashioned of the same impenetrable void. With a shaky hand, Tony reached out, fingers nervously descending into the dark sack. After a minute of rooting around, his hand withdrew, holding a blue plastic sphere. Staring at the cheap plastic in disbelief, he mumbled a thank you before moving to transfer the sphere to his bucket.

One hand snapped out, pointing a gnarled finger at him.

"Wait."

He didn't need to be told twice. He remained motionless as Janey and Elle each took their turn. Janey got a green capsule, yellow for Elle.

The withered hands receded into the black shroud, taking the bag with them. Barely a moment later, they reemerged, palms up and empty. The fingers flourished in a wave before producing a red sphere from nowhere. Elle, teetering on horrified, couldn't help but be impressed.

The gnarled hands surrounded the ball on two hemispheres before squeezing. The ball made a splintering noise, then separated into two halves like a plastic egg. The hands raised the two halves before turning them over. Something viscous and dark dripped out, splattering onto the walkway. The two halves followed, clattering against the concrete steps, discarded.

"Open."

The hands insisted, gesturing as the kids looked at one another, mimicking the gesture seen. The sound echoed as three containers split in unison.

"Ew." Janey mewed, dropping the halves on the ground, and wiping the slimy mess from her hands onto her lab coat.

"Yuck," Tony uttered as a similar dark ichor dripped out of his sphere. He tried to drop the halves, but they clung to his gloves.

Elle parted her halves, but nothing came out. As she raised her pieces to inspect closer, something shifted in one half. With a quick shuffle, she reached into the cup and withdrew an unfamiliar shape.

It took forever for her eyes to adjust, even in the bright light around her. Perhaps that was her brain's way of delaying the inevitable reaction of holding a desiccated bird skull between her fingers. She shrieked, dropping the tiny skull; her horror momentary, discarded in the confusion of billowing fabric and shadowy laughter.

Instinct forced them back two steps, looking in all directions. The street was still as empty as it had been when they agreed this was the last house. The fires around them glowed brighter, then dimmed again as the laughter subsided.

Janey grabbed at Elle with her free hand, taking another step back. Elle turned to make eye contact, confusion visible on her face. They looked toward Tony, but he was still staring. Above them and beyond explanation, the shadow held a gnarled horn. One end receded into the darkness, the rest widening and twisting perversely as it curled open and outward into the night. It was not the horn of any animal seen on Earth. Its sound was deafening, panic and fear rising in its wake. Two blasts – one short, one long, and the horn disappeared in a flurry of black.

The kids could do nothing but stare confused as they each fought against the fear that was building inside them.

"Run."

The word was barely coughed out before the shadow collapsed in on itself, leaving only a billow of fabric on the stoop. As if in reply, a howl resounded in the distance, wisping through the trees to echo around them on the sidewalk.

"What the –" Tony looked between the pile of fabric and the far-flung spaces where the howl reached from.

"We're leaving," Janey tugged at Tony and Elle, dragging them away from the porch.

She stepped off the path, manners abandoning her as she crossed the lawn, seeking the shortest distance between here and home. She tugged until her friends fell in step, moving from stumble to jog. She tried to ignore the uneven ground cover as she increased her gait, but it got worse the further they traveled. The lawn was shifting beneath them!

Janey screamed as she fell in the grass. In the light from the porch, they could see the hand that held fast to her shoe. One hand among dozens rising out of the lawn.

Tony and Elle paused to pull Janey to her feet. Together they hop-skipped frantically across the green space, kicking over the warning and finding momentary refuge on the city sidewalk.

Panting, they held each other, even as they ushered one another on, looking back only for a moment as the ground split in a dozen places, hulking forms lurching up out of the dirt.

"We gotta go." Tony rasped between heaving breaths, pushing the two girls down the sidewalk.

Janey pointed to one house, then another. Porch lights were off, but the doors were all open. Standing in the thresholds were the dark shape of each house's occupant, two small pinpoints of light glowing where eyes might be. The lights followed the children down the street, never venturing from their doorways.

"What's happening?" Elle couldn't mask her panic. No one dared to respond.

A howl ripped through the air, the accompanying breeze rustling the leaves above as if the howl was a force of its own. By the time it reached the trio in the middle of the street, the sound was everywhere, ringing in their ears. There was no way to determine its origin.

Janey clenched her friends' hands. "Which way?"

Eyes flicked in every direction, looking for a path to or from. Elle grabbed their hands, pulling them down the street that looked most familiar. The truth was nothing in Woodfield looked familiar in this much darkness.

Neighbors emerged from their houses, spaced along the sidewalks, pinpoints tracking the kids as they ran. Each stared with hollow eyes, jaws unhinged to a painful extreme, a soft blue glow emanating from the back of their throats. Everyone saw it; no one spoke about it.

They ran until all they could hear was thundering heartbeats and rasping breath. They waited, listening. One by one, they dropped to the asphalt, relief momentary as they broke down together.

Janey blubbered between gasps for air.

"Why is this happening to us? What did we do?"

"We got greedy," Tony whispered; his Halloween bucket, like the girls', abandoned blocks earlier.

The girls stared at him, neither attempting to correct him. The explanation made sense, even if there was no explaining any of it rationally.

Another howl interrupted their revelation. The trio huddled close together, attempting to block out the earth-shattering sound. Silence followed almost as abruptly. Tony didn't hesitate, tugging on both of their hands.

"Come on!"

The gecko head bobbed frantically as he tried to pull them along. It jerked around, mirth long gone from the motion, even as the hulking shape struck Tony, pinning him down on the street. The girls screamed with Tony as he thrashed under the mass of black fur that pawed at him.

Elle clambered forward, grabbing one of Tony's kicking feet and pulled. She tugged once and the thing lurched, tugging back. She pulled again, groaning, and felt Tony slip between its thick furred legs. On the third try, she lost her footing and fell back, a ripping sound making her stomach lurch.

Tony rolled, a sweaty mop of hair framing panicked eyes as he scrambled out from under the creature. They watched the beast's frothing maw rip and chew his mother's handiwork.

They said nothing, knowing they only had a minute before the creature realized. Instead, they darted in the opposite direction, taking the first turn they found to break the line of sight, extending their survival a second at a time.

The creature roared its frustration when it realized the real prey had slipped away. Fingers clenched tighter, holding each other close by as they ran faster, no destination in mind except away.

Behind them, lumbering and snarling grew louder, the distance closing quickly under thunderous strides.

They were so focused on the creature bearing down on them from behind that they didn't even notice the one blocking their escape. It hissed like a razor, slashing its way through the children without breaking stride. Elle's grip broke free of the others, spinning her as she ran, trying to keep her feet.

They didn't stop – didn't dare – but chanced a glance behind. The hulking mass of creature tumbled, thrashing and howling as if under attack. It struggled, clambering before falling in a heap. It tried to pull itself upright once more but collapsed again in a wheeze. The children paused to see another being dislodge itself from the beast. It barely turned its attention to them before it had already closed the distance. There wasn't enough time to scream let alone run.

Separated from the group like easy prey, Elle was the

obvious choice. She screamed for her life as it drove her to the asphalt, tumbling with her, sharp claws holding her fast. They came to rest with it on top of her, holding her down and hissing again as it opened its maw. Elle twisted away from the rows of teeth blossoming forth as its jaw unhinged.

"Elle!"

The thing turned for a moment to hiss a threat at Janey and Tony. Elle struggled, but the talons clenched, encouraging her to remain. Still, she cried out one last time.

"Run!"

The creature whirled on her, its lamprey mouth choking on a hiss as it loomed. The fan of teeth folded, flesh concealing them as burning eyes regarded her.

"Elle?"

The sound was cavernous, her name lost within it, barely recognizable. But when death paused above her, she couldn't help but meet the creature's gaze. A nightmarish maw and gargoyle skin stared wide-eyed. Flesh stitched itself back together, stone flaking away as hair sprouted. Somewhere in the mask of horror was a trace of humanity.

Not just humanity, but a face Elle knew.

"Mom?"

Red eyes were all that remained of the monster as Elle's mother crouched over her, half-naked and pulling her daughter into a deep hug as tears began to flow.

"I... didn't know."

"I –" Elle stuttered; their moment interrupted by a deep growl up the street.

Her mom put a hand to her daughter's cheek, a smile

attempting to conceal the wince of pain as her fingertips split, claws emerging. She stood, turning her back to the kids.

"Run home."

It was two syllables, but in the space between them, familiarity vanished. The sound was hollow, hungry. Flesh sloughed off stone as spines sprouted from her shoulders.

Tony and Janey swept in, pulling Elle away from the scene. Even as they ran, Elle couldn't bring herself to look away, the shape of her mother all but lost in the shifting form of the creature that stood between three children and a hulking beast. A shape that almost consumed them itself.

Screeches and howls followed them to the boulevard, where, even back among the crowds of candy seekers, none of them felt safe in the dark.

They stood beneath a streetlight in full view of a cop car as they watched the mouth of the Woodfield neighborhood. Thirty minutes passed, the cold chill of the dropping temperature replacing the ominous chill Woodfield provided. They only decided to move when the crowds thinned enough that they felt exposed.

Together, they trudged, until the soundscape held no hostility, until shadows held no threat. They shuffled until the neighborhoods around them held no secrets. Pausing as a single entity, they looked along the intersection. Janey lived up; Elle's house was down; Tony was further down and a little over. None of the paths home allowed them to travel together much further. They held hands, each stretching to arm's length, searching for the courage to let go and run home.

They were still there, fingers intertwined, when the police collected them an hour later at the behest of two frantic phone calls. The third call never came. Though parents and police alike asked repeatedly, Elle didn't know how to tell them where her mom was tonight, or why she wasn't answering her phone.

Good Horror

Jenifer Lynn

"No one appreciates good horror anymore."

I looked up from my coffee at the old man sitting alone two tables down. He was hunched against the window in an oversized coat, sparse and unkempt white hair stuck out from under a battered gray homburg that looked like it had been on his head since the last time it was in fashion. His cheeks were weathered and cut through with deep lines, a treasure map to decades of joy and sadness.

His attention was turned to the street outside where gangs of costumed children poured through the artery of the street, coagulating at doorways to push through and into businesses offering sweets and treats.

"Where are the wolfmen and the vampires? The spooky ghosts?" he was speaking to no one, but everyone, his words stunted with a slight accent that I couldn't place. Russian, maybe? "It's the movies. All they do is blood and torture. These kids dress up like serial killers who have no style beyond hack and slash."

The bell above the door rang sharp as a blob of children oozed into the cafe, shouting and laughing. The old man was right. Not a single witch or goblin. A couple superheroes, to be expected after the year's summer blockbusters. One young princess, clinging desperately to an older brother's hand to avoid being pulled into the current of moving bodies. But mostly the old man had it pegged. A death mask, the signature headwear from the most recent slasher flick. There were other costumes from older movies, a serial killer that used a hatchet and a chainsaw, and another one that dressed in a bright green plastic tuxedo when he dealt the final blow.

The classics were missing.

The children swarmed the register where an exhausted waitress doled out candy to the invaders. Glittering alien eyeballs bobbed on top of her head as she nodded at each child, cooing about their costumes. The princess fought through to the front, her pudgy fist holding up a golden pumpkin bucket. Her voice was loud and well-rehearsed as she shouted above the cacophony. "Twick or Tweet!" The woman's smile grew larger, more genuine, as she tossed an extra candy bar into the princess' bucket. As they left and silence again crept into the cafe, I turned back to the old man.

"Slasher films can be scary, too," I said.

The man eyed me, waving a leathery hand in the air in dismissal. "They're too boring to be scary. No depth. Just hack hack hack." The hand made slashing motions in the air. "There's no poetry to it."

"Poetry?" I asked, motioning to the waitress for a refill on my coffee. Glitter from her headband left a light dust on the table, a few pieces landing on the black sludge she poured into my cup. I smiled and nodded a thank you, trying and failing to fish the pieces out before they sank.

"Yes, poetry. The unbridled anger of the werewolf, the devious magic of the witch, the desperate tragedy of the ghost. A poetry and depth to the characters that gave them life and made them all the more terrifying." The waitress poured coffee and glitter into his cup and he waved in her direction before taking a sip.

"And the vampires?" I asked. "What's their poetry?"

The man smiled, the lines of his face deepening. "The most poetic of all," he said. "A never ending cycle, having to kill to maintain their own life, their youth. The constant question of whether or not the sacrifice of another, maybe even an innocent, is worth their continued existence."

I cocked my head to the side, studying him. "So, fictional serial killers don't scare you, and that's fair," I said. "But what about the real ones?"

A plate of glittering fries appeared on my table. "I think serial killers are super scary," the waitress piped as she moved to the old man's table and set an order of toast in front of him. "Especially right now. That one that's been killing off the homeless people in the city." She shivered and wrapped her arms around herself. "Makes me afraid to go home at night."

"My dear," the old man said, dipping his toast into his coffee, "that sentence alone makes me think you ought not be afraid of the Transient Killer."

"What do you mean?" she asked, eyes wide under her bobbling headband.

"He kills homeless people..." he said, the thin thread of his patience visibly stretching in the lines above one raised eyebrow. "You're going home..."

A moment later she laughed. "Oh, right!" She laughed again, patting the old man's shoulder. "You've got a point, and I need another coffee, apparently." She returned to the register as another glut of costumed children squeezed through the door and pooled around her, reaching and shouting. I tuned out the noise, turning my focus to my french fries, tapping them one by one on the plate to dislodge the green glitter.

A few moments later the trick-or-treaters were gone again, and I turned my attention back to the old man. He was stuffing the last bits of coffee-soaked toast into his mouth, brown liquid dribbling down his chin.

"What about you," I continued our conversation. "Are you afraid of real life serial killers?"

He wiped his chin with a dirty, crusty sleeve. "Pathetic," he said. "Even more than the ones in the movies." He tipped his mug up, pouring what was bound to be a buttery, glittery sludge into his mouth and swallowing. "At least in the movies they've got some sort of supernatural bent. Real serial killers are simply whiny babies looking for attention." The lines in his face twisted like a tragedy mask as his voice climbed two octaves. "Oh, Mommy didn't love me. Oh, Daddy abused me. Oh, I was *so* traumatized, wah wah wah." He slammed his palm on the table. "There's nothing interesting there, nothing novel, just pathetic sons of bitches who should have found a good therapist."

I pushed the remainder of my sparkling fries to the side. "That seems oversimplified, don't you think?"

He dusted his hands off on the front of his shirt. "Nope."

I nodded and stood, pulling a couple bills from my wallet. "I've got your coffee, friend. Did you want a slice of pie?"

The old man frowned. "I don't need your charity, or your pie."

I smiled, "Well don't have the pie, then." I gestured to the waitress to ring us both up at the register, whispering, "add the pie." She nodded and handed me the change, which I dropped in the tip jar before turning back to the old man. "I wish you both the happiest of Halloweens."

The waitress waved and chirped "Happy Halloween!" as I left. The old man grumbled and kept his eyes on me through the window as I walked down the street, swept along by the flow of trick-or-treaters until I was out of his line of sight.

***

It was almost an hour before the old man left the diner.

The costumed commotion from earlier had been replaced with a hushed October mist that cooled and cleansed the glitter and frivolity from the streets. I had watched from my perch in the alley one block down from the diner as the children dissipated, scattering to parent's cars as the rain hit, make-up smearing on their cheeks.

I was soaked to the bone by the time he came out, and I wondered if he had taken me up on the pie afterall. He looked right, then left. He squinted in my direction, but there was no way he would have seen me, stuck firmly in the shadows. He shrugged, his filthy coat moving stiffly around him, and chose the left path, moving in my direction.

A part of me was disappointed. I had hoped he would turn right, challenging me to follow. I'd have to cross in front of the diner again without the waitress seeing me. To catch up to him before he turned down another alley, but without being noticed. I loved the challenge. But that wasn't my *favorite* part.

I reached under my jacket, feeling the bone handle of my knife, warm and waiting. I slipped it from its sheath and felt it heat up in my hand as the old man's footsteps grew closer. It was always so easy, a smooth motion, lunge into the light and drag them back to the shadows. Maybe a slight struggle, but always the spray of blood as my knife slid across their necks.

This man was no different. His breath smelled of coffee and cherry pie as I held him to me, watching the blood splatter onto the brick wall, before it slowed, dribbling down his front to pool at his feet. Careful to avoid the mess, I held him away from me, and let him fall to the ground. He landed on his side, the motion rolling him onto his back. His eyes were open, some life still left in them, and I stood above him so he could see me.

"Are you scared now?" I asked him as I wiped the blade of my knife on his sleeve.

The old man coughed, blood trickling from his mouth as a smile curved his lips.

***

I was nearly home, trudging through a broken down

neighborhood that would hopefully soon surrender to gentrification, when I heard the footsteps. Casually I turned to look behind me. A vagrant, covered in rags, slipped behind an overflowing dumpster. I heard it slump to the ground, the sound of a glass bottle hitting the sidewalk with it. The knife against my ribs hummed, but I ignored it. There was a hot tea and a shot of whiskey waiting to chase away the chill of the rain just a few blocks away. There would be other nights.

The shadowing footsteps began again the moment I started back on my path. A second echo bouncing off the burnt out buildings and alleys around me, muted by the heavy mists, but still there. I spun again, seeing another bundle of rags and filth slink from the shadows. This one stood for a moment, watching me, before it sank to its hands and knees.

Movement on the opposite side of the street drew my attention, the first vagrant was pulling itself on top of the dumpster it had ducked behind. A worn blanket wrapped around its head like a hood hid its face from view, but I felt its eyes on me as it settled into a crouch.

Both figures, now completely still, completely focused on me. The hilt of my knife burned hot as anger drove away the first flicker of fear. Filthy vagrants. Disgusting transients.

Another noise, this time on a fire escape above me. This

vagrant, less than ten feet from my head, pressed itself flat against the metal grate, dirty fingers reaching through. I could see this one's eyes buried within its layers of muddy cloth, glittering dark and intent on me.

The other two, a half block away, had begun to move. One crawled along the sidewalk, low to the ground like a lizard, slow and steady. The other leapt from its perch on the dumpster, reached the hanging ladder of a fire escape and pulled itself up and into the maze of grates, slithering through the bars.

I turned my attention back up to the third and found it had dropped from the fire escape, hanging upside down, its face directly above me. It opened dirty, crusted lips and hissed, "Are you scared now?"

The question was echoed in the misty air, first from the two that were slowly encroaching, but then other voices, unseen in the alleys and shadows.

I drew my knife, the comforting weight of it hollow in my hand, and backed away from the vagrants I could see, scanning the street for the ones I couldn't. I spun slowly in place, seeing shadows move unnaturally from every alley, every broken window. Completely surrounded.

When I completed my turn, the original three creatures were only a few yards away, now joined by others, slinking and slithering along the sidewalks and walls. The whispering hiss, "Are you scared now?" overlapped by tittering, croaking, laughter. Anger flared and fizzled, replaced irreparably by fear. I sheathed my knife with tingling fingers, and ran, the thundering of my heartbeat not enough to drown out the whispers and laughter. Only six blocks and I would be home. I could almost see the glow of my neighborhood past these abandoned buildings and broken streetlights. My lungs burned against the chilled mist that filled them, but I would make it if I ran fast enough.

A figure stepped out of the alley ahead, flanked immediately by low, crawling indigents, blocking my way forward.

The old man smiled at me from a pale, drawn face, blood coagulated on the front of his oversized coat. His eyes flashed silver and he hissed, the wound at his throat bubbling with the effort, "Am I afraid now?"

In one smooth motion he lunged, grabbing me and pulling me back into the shadows of the alley. I struggled, grasping at the arm that held me around the torso, the hot bone handle of my knife digging into my ribs. The blood that drenched him, cold and sticky, seeped through my jacket and shirt. The other figures, more and more of them, gathered at the alley entrance, bobbing and swaying while they watched. The old man's breath, still smelling of acrid coffee and cherry pie, was warm against my cheek as he croaked, "Nope."

I didn't think to scream until his fangs pierced my neck, digging deep and crushing my larynx.

Sometime later I felt myself falling to the ground, the pain a dull, slowing throb through my entire body. I felt the old man turn me over, and saw him hovering over me. Fresh blood covered his chin, dripping down to mix with the older blood on his coat. As I watched, the lines of his face softened and receded. The white wispy hair on his head thickened and grew dark.

"There may be a bit of poetry in your story after all," he spoke in a voice decades younger than it had been an hour previous. He shrugged off his filthy coat and crouched over me, smiling with a now youthful grin as he tucked it under my head. The vignette of impending oblivion pinpointed my vision, but I could still see the rest of the creatures, glittering eyed and dripping fanged, as they drew nearer.

"But only this bit at the end."

Midnight Snack

Andy Lockwood

It was baffling. That wasn't a word Jase was accustomed to using, but that's exactly what it was. He was standing – alright, he was kneeling – on a patch of dirt and grass underneath an old-growth tree... in the middle of the warehouse district. He rubbed his eyes and looked up at the thing again. The leaves on the underside of the canopy were still green. Brittle, perhaps, but the color was still there. They faded into yellows, oranges, and reds as the canopy rose above the buildings that surrounded it. At the top, there were some dry browns, but most of the dead leaves had been scattered already by the late October winds.

Late October, Jase laughed. *Very late. Minutes to go.*

The last time he looked at the clock, it read 11:23 PM. That was about the time he turned the corner, the brick opening into a yard of untouched greenspace in the middle of a rusted-out factory.

Baffling.

He opened his duffle, organizing its contents around him. Time was running out for Jase, its passage a coil around his heart, twisting, tightening. He knew he had until midnight, but it felt like midnight might be too late.

The breeze picked up again, painting his fevered skin with goosebumps. He squinted; his eyes peppered with grit from the alley. It wasn't worth guessing what was sticking to him. He put his mind elsewhere; it had been a long October, but things were finally coming to a head.

Jase paused his rummaging. Stuffing a pinky finger in his ear, he twisted it around and listened again. The wind whispered between the walls around him, leaves and waste rustling across the grounds, but nothing else caught his attention. He could have sworn he heard laughter.

He shrugged it off. The warehouse district was far flung from the welcoming residential neighborhoods that hosted trick-or-treaters tonight. Children had torn up and down his block all evening, scavenging candy and other treats from anyone who dared open their door. But as far as the children were concerned, Halloween ended hours ago. October 31st was just another day to the high brick walls of the industrial complex; unobserved and ignored, much like the treasure hidden somewhere within.

There was a scuttle behind him. He spun on his knees, holding the strap of his bag in one hand like a whip, while thumbing the flashlight on. He panted, his jaw tensing; something scurried in the dark, just out of sight of the flashlight beam. Jase scanned the area again; nothing but shadows cast by the patches of tall grass.

He positioned the light and flipped open the book. He'd read the passage plenty of times, knew it practically by heart, but didn't want to miss a word. This was his moment; his opportunity to change everything. Jase wasn't going to mess it up.

Everyone else looked to New Year's Eve as a chance to start clean, but Jase's opportunity was Halloween. At least, that's what the book told him.

Jase had a shelf of trophies he collected from various purse snatchings and carjackings. Anything unique and interesting was put up on the shelf for later. When he was high, he'd pull something down and puzzle it out. He didn't have much use for books, but this one was interesting. Leather bound and past vintage, he almost didn't notice the wispy hairs in the leather at first. Or the way the symbols and letters on the cover didn't look printed – they looked tattooed.

The text was foreign, but the notes scrawled between the lines were clear enough. The book covered a bunch of things he didn't understand and couldn't pronounce, but one passage caught his eye. The spine was cracked at this page, the paper barely holding to the seam, both outside corners dogeared, and notes written in all the margins.

Wish magic: conjure anything you desire with a strong wish and a small sacrifice.

He turned the page, curious; a crumpled piece of plain

paper fell into his lap. Written in the same scrawl were an address and a date: *Halloween.* Jase laughed, *Of course the spell should be cast on Halloween.* He didn't put it down though. Sure, he was high, but it didn't mean it wasn't worth checking out. Halloween was only a couple weeks away, after all. So began the collection of ingredients, understanding the steps, and, finally, finding the damn place.

Jase set out the plate, then unwrapped the raw steak he stole on the way over.

There was another rustle in the grass. He paused, waiting, certain a stray had caught the scent of meat. Great. He didn't want interruptions during the ritual, but maybe if he got to the recitation, he could scare the animal off.

He opened the book, then the small baggie. He sprinkled the contents over the hunk of meat, then reached for the lighter fluid and the lighter. Careful not to spray on the dish, he poured the accelerant in a circle, and then lit it up.

The burst of flame temporarily blinded him, but he didn't falter. He'd all but memorized the pages. He picked up the knife, closing a fist around the blade, and pulled hard with the other hand.

Jase drew a breath and tried not to curse out – he had no idea if that would jinx the ritual – but it was hard to breathe through the pain that engulfed his hand. Trying to push it aside, he held his fist over the plate and squeezed, counting to himself as blood poured between his closed fingers, bathing the raw meat beneath.

Another deep breath, and he opened his throat, ready to call to the heavens.

"Dark lord, I beseech –" He began, but paused abruptly, interrupted by keening laughter. It echoed off the walls around him, sounding like a hundred voices. He got to his feet; knife clenched in his good hand.

"Dark lord," a voice parroted. It was shrill but gravelly, its words followed by an eruption of laughter.

Jase held the knife out, twisting around, uncertain where to direct his defense. He reached down and grabbed the flashlight, swinging it the beam in a path opposite the knife. The laughter quieted, a rush of whispers swirling around him like dead leaves chasing the wind.

"I accept."

Turning, Jase pointed the beam of light at the tree, watching as the deep grooves of the old bark shifted, separating from the tree until something stood, stepping away from the tree itself. It was enormous, standing on stilt legs, a crown of gnarled antlers shedding leaves with each heavy step. Its skin was a mosaic of dark shadow and white bone; aged bark that had seen more than its share of seasons.

It stepped closer, Jase craning his neck upward, his brain unable to process the full spectacle before him. The laughter erupted around him again and he saw smaller creatures perched on the larger one; they were compact bundles of shadow, watching him through beady pinpoints of light, and laughing through mouthfuls of sharp, glistening teeth.

In a singular moment of clarity, Jase processed as much of the scene as he could, formulating a simple, but reasonable reply.

"I didn't say my wish."

It knelt, still towering over Jase, examining him. Its body creaked like old tree limbs bending in the wind, the sound descending into a growl that terrified Jase.

"It's not your wish," its voice reverberated through Jase, echoing in his bones. Around them, the laughter rolled gently in the tall grass, encircling them. "You are the sacrifice."

Jase felt the cold trail of a single tear running down his cheek. He didn't bother to raise the knife in defense. His knees were too weak to run away. But his lungs were plenty capable, screaming out to the heavens as the first mouthful of teeth sank into his flesh.

The Last Samhain

Jess Boldt

The young woman muffled her exclamation of pain as a thorned branch from the undergrowth tore at her leg. She pushed her bare feet harder against rock, moss, and grass; each stride more painful, more powerful than the one before. Each push forced her long copper hair to briefly cover her vision but there was no time to clear that particular obstacle from her view. She knew the land only from brief memories of childhood and while the sunset changed that land to be more unrecognizable, she tore through the forest's shadows, her fear, her absolute terror honed keen her senses and negated the unfamiliar terrain. Her senses were too sharp, in fact, she could feel the wet blood draw from her wound, pool, and drip down her leg and ankle. Each thud of her heart between deep desperate breaths pushed the crimson with more force from the cut, but she dared not stop or even rest because she knew something was chasing her. Hunting her. And it knew her name. *Mairenn.*

Her lungs drew in choking heat only to sputter out half the air they claimed. The vision that had been finely attuned with fear had now begun to sparkle with bright white lights. Maireen shook her head and drew in the fire of breath even deeper, all the while suppressing the instinct to stop, cough, and vomit. There, in the far distance past branches, thickets and thorns, a spark of light different from the floating phantasms brought on by lack of air. The first sign of the birth of a distant bonfire, her destination. It was too far too small, her body carried her past her limits, desperately away from the hooves of her pursuer's mount. Every muscle begged her to seize the flight and give in to relief, no matter how brief. She let out a silent scream of rebellion against her being and pushed harder. With each stubborn, agonizing stride, the light of the bonfire grew slowly closer, now blurred with burning tears.

Every stone, patch of vegetation Mairenn's feet sprung from were met by the thunderous sound of horse hooves soon after. Her left leg froze for a fraction of a moment, its muscles twisted beyond the force of will. This event was followed by her right foot hitting a stone, instead of the needed friction, it was met with the wet blood from her cut, sending her sideways, tumbling towards the ground below. Time and the universe slowed around her. The gradient orange blue of sunset had become a static point in the sky. Although her mind processed the fall in tedious moments, her exhausted body refused to react. She felt a final tightening of her muscles as she braced, as best she could, for the impact of flesh against ground. Just as she gave herself to the coming blunt impact and the fate that traveled fast on horseback behind her. The world spun in flashes of sky and foliage, and just as she was ready to cede consciousness, she felt her body slam into something that gave way and cushion to her fall. She gasped for air only to have her mouth silenced by a hand until the black horse raced past her location and deeper into the long shadows of the trees ahead.

Her mind rushed to panic, but only found fatigue. She gasped into the hand until it was finally removed by its owner. She sat up straight and drew in a loud breath. Another one, her vision softened as she focused on the young man who sat down in front of her. The color of his shoulder length hair was impossible to make out with her diminished vision. She coughed and nearly sicked as her lungs sputtered to find purchase of air. The young man brushed some vagrant strands of hair from his forehead and looked up towards the distant sound of hooves against terrain. He then turned his attention to her.

"Breath slowly, you'll be fine," the young man said. "I think he was just going in for a bit of a scare and went too far, but you can't be too careful."

Mairenn clutched her chest, feeling her ribs move more regular with each inhale. She looked down and noticed her hand shaking against her breasts. "We have to get out of here. It, it called my name," she cried as she concentrated on her breathing.

"Probably just some jealous suitor or someone drunk on spoiled wine," the young man replied.

"I, I swear I heard him scream my name. It was Gan Ceann himself, come to claim my life, I'm for sure doomed," she sobbed.

The man laughed gently and shook his head. "The day's festivities have gotten to your head. Gan Ceann, indeed. Trust me, there aren't any gods or other such wandering this forsaken bog land, I can assure you that. Just drunkards, whether it be on the wine or on conviction. I would bet that coward of a man is of the cross and saw you heading towards the mounds. Thought he would give you a bit of a scare."

Mairenn's face began to burn with anger as she forgot the fear that had made sport of her system moments earlier. She flung her hands up high and just as quickly put her palms to the ground. "I know what I have heard. He, he called my name, I have to make it to the fire," She braced herself and stood up.

"You're injured," the man observed.

"It's a cut, and I ran with it fine and I'll walk with it just as fine," she replied. And she did. "Just because you were so noble to catch me in the act of falling doesn't mean I need you to dote on me. I'm grateful for your assistance, but I really must reach that village," she said, not unkindly, but determined as she walked herself down the path.

"Catch you, is that what you call it? You flung yourself at me, for which I'm grateful or I would have surely been trampled by that drunkard. Either way, don't think of me as some hero to the rescue. I was just out for a walk, something about the air this evening," he said as he looked down at her bloodied foot. "The bleeding should slow, but you should take it easy on that foot. And perhaps the trail isn't the best route, our friend may return if he gets bored or decides to bite another cork."

Maireen bent down and tore off a line of cloth from her dress. She then proceeded to wrap her cut then stood, staring down the path. She brushed her hair out of her eyes and wiped them with her forearm. "I swear, he called my name, but I just feel empty right now, numb."

"A person only has so much fear at a time, and it looks like you burnt through yours like dry kindling. Don't get too comfortable, it'll return once your constitution returns. That said, we should probably take a lesser known path. Perhaps through the bogs."

"I remember those old wooden roads as a child, and to cross over them this evening would be dangerous," she replied.

"Aye, not the steadiest of paths, but one that no horse would take, not in their condition," the man replied.

"You really don't believe that rider to be of spirit, do you?" she asked.

"Not at all. The only things about this night are flesh and blood people and the things that those of flesh and blood create. Most are honest, but some are more trouble than their weight," he replied.

Maireen, now of regular breath and composure, was able to focus more on the man. He wore a loose fitting traveler's shirt made from a lightly dyed wool cloth. She noticed this first, for the material seemed to rest easy, almost weightless on his shoulders where dark hair came to the end of its length. His eyes, dark brown in color and kind in shape and depth. She suddenly became self-conscious, for in observing him, she knew he was observing her. She quickly brushed her light copper hair that reflected the setting sun out of her face.

"My name is Maireen, I am traveling to see my uncle, the village to the north there," she said as she pointed to the flame in the distance. "I was separated from my travel party in the fog, hours before that mad man had set upon me."

"My friends call me Thrush, so I suppose you are welcome to do the same," he stated.

Maireen laughed then caught herself and adjusted to a quieter giggle. "Like the bird?"

"Like the bird," Thrush replied.

"Well, then, uh, Thrush, would it be an inconvenience to travel with me to the festivities, through the bogs?"

"I think that would be a fine idea, Maireen," he replied.

She walked herself from the trodden path, past thistle and thorn, down the hill that led to an old wooden path made of oak plank that stretched far into the wetlands.

Each step on the oaken path caused the ground to sway gently. At first Maireen's steps were short and careful as she watched Thrush slow down to keep her pace. The setting sun shimmered on the water, chorused by the soft sound of the remaining wildlife singing their autumn requiem. She soon found herself striding behind Thrush with equal confidence.

"I remember, as a child, this place was more lively. There were the voices of so many frogs, and other creatures. It feels lesser now, at least from my memories," Maireen noted.

"Most of the frogs have begun their winter sleep, but there's still plenty of life here. You've mentioned that you used to live here as a child. I take it that you have been gone for some time then," Thrush inquired.

"Twelve years, I believe," she replied.

"To the sea then? The city?"

"Aye, how did you know?"

Thrush shook his head and looked back at Maireen. "It's the sea air. There's no mistaking it, and it clings to everyone who has spent enough time there. Not just the fragrance of salt, mind you. It's the wind that has traveled a hundred shores, sunk a thousand ships. There's a story in every breeze."

"So, you've been to the sea, yourself?" Maireen inquired.

"I've been all over, really. Family all over this country," Thrush stated while turning his attention back to the boarded road. "So, what brings you back to this remote place? Not enough adventure?"

Marieen looked out towards the last remnants of the sun's influence as the waters seemed to glow red with the reflection. "Growing up, my father would tell me stories of creatures who he saw as a child. Stories of the old times where priests held grand celebrations to honor and fear the invisible world. Stories of the Aos sí, and the old gods. He would tell me what he saw, and experienced here."

"Isn't the stick guy enough of a god for you," Thrush inquired.

"Stick guy?"

Thrush stopped and turned around to face Maireen. He outstretched his hands to both sides and slumped his head downward to his chest. The young woman gasped for a moment then threw her hand over her mouth to prevent him from seeing her startled smile.

"You know, you would get right beaten for talking about Christ like that if the wrong person saw you," she said, unable to tamp down her surprised amusement.

"Well, are you saying he isn't your god?" Thrush inquired.

"I guess he's God to us all, at least that is what is proper and expected thought. But you should have heard my father's stories. They were so much more compelling than the morality tales of a thousand years ago about places I would never visit. Please don't think I am a blasphemer, I just think there's more room in this world than what the church states as fact," Maireen said, blushing at the awareness of her long withheld honesty.

Thrush laughed and smiled. "I am in no position to accuse a soul of blasphemy, nor would I ever want such responsibilities. You know, there's a tale from the very village we're heading towards. A few hundred years ago, when the night was celebrated with more, well, authenticity. When the shadow of the stone steeples were just beginning to stretch onto this land. Well, I suppose that story will have to wait. We still have a bit before the festival, and the night has all but taken over."

Maireen paused her steps and looked out over the bog and back towards the light of the bonfire, which had not only increased in size as they closed the distance, but was now more illuminated as the sun sank past the horizon. She sighed, "You can tell it to me as we make our way. I would love to hear more of the history of this place. In a way, it's a part of my history as well. We can afford to slow our pace a bit," she said as Thrush began his tale.

"A few hundred years ago, the chief of this village was a holy man in his own right, as many of them were. They kept the old ways and were true to their gods. As a matter of fact, if you were to reverse time and rebuild this road, you would have offshoots that led to the testament of their devotion to some of these gods. This chief, Domhnall, kept to the old ways despite the growing influence that came by sea and sword. However, his brother, Ruarcc was an early convert to the new religion. He was so taken by the tenets of the cross that he grew to become an abbot and traveled, preaching salvation and absolution to all ready ears. Now, one would think that this would create quite the chasm for the two brothers, however, every night of this very festival, Ruarcc would visit his old village. Not necessarily to convert, but to engage in deep dialogues with his brother about the nature of the universe, the validity of their beliefs against each other's arguments. This would go far into the night, and sometimes into the morning. One night they argued about a story of some man named Judas, who betrayed the stick god, I mean Jesus, of course. Whether he was just in fulfilling a prophecy of some sort or if he was just a traitor meant for damnation. Another time, they discussed the nature of hypocrisy in using religious justification to conquer lands far away from here. To most, these would have been very boorish discussions, especially when there was a feast with wine and song just footsteps outside of the straw thatched hut. But for two men like that, it was the perfect time, as they had both known the sacredness of the festival, and they saw no better way to honor those departed spirits than through such conversations."

As Maireen listened, she shook her head as she began to see the slightest blurs of lights rise from the blog. She shut her eyes tight, and took a deep breath. Thrush stopped and walked towards her, placing his hand on her shoulder. "Are you alright?"

She opened her eyes, seeing just the darkness of the night. "It's nothing, My vision is still recovering. Please continue," she said assuredly.

"If you insist," he said as he removed his hand and resumed his slow pace. "As I was saying, most people would have thought these conversations rather dull. But there was one creature who found them absolutely fascinating. A boy of sorts, but this boy was not human, but of the invisible world, as the tale has been told to me. In fact, he was most often not a boy. He was a púca."

Maireen gasped in delighted recognition.

"His favorite form was of a rabbit, fast and nimble. But he often loved taking the form of a young boy during the festival times. He could dart unseen by the people of the village, sneak their food and drink, play their games, but his favorite diversion was sitting close to Domnhall's hut, listening as the two priests talked just loud enough for him to eavesdrop. For the next couple of years, he would make sure to listen to their stories, often desiring to sit in and offer up his own naive opinions. However, this would have been a mistake.

A few years later, both priests were older, and more rooted into their roles. They went long into the night after a discussion regarding what they knew of the viking theology that had been springing up on coastal settlements. Ruarcc was convinced that they were well on their way to bowing to his religion. Well, as the boy, the púca listened, he forgot himself and shifted into his real form. To most humans, a frightening and unnatural form of an unholy mix of nature and man.

"It was around this time that Ruarcc decided to relieve himself next to the hut. To his surprise, he came upon this creature. At that moment, something changed in the man. You see, in his theology, there could have only been one real explanation for this thing's existence. It most certainly was a demon brought up from damnation itself. He pulled out a small dagger and swiped at it, cutting its cheek. The poor creature was pulled out of the spell brought on by the conversation, and he screamed and ran into the forest, now taking flight as the fastest rabbit ever seen in these lands.

"It wasn't until later the creature found out what consequences his mere existence had on the world. For it was later learned that Ruarcc's mind had indeed broken at the sight of it. He quickly reasoned, in a fit of fear and delirium, that Domhnall was in league with the devil and he had been a guilty party by merely visiting him and indulging in conversation. He gripped his dagger more tightly and went into the hut, demanding Domhnall convert right there and then. Those that overheard the commotion said that Domhnall just laughed, thinking it a joke until the blade plunged into his stomach, then heart. Some who heard the scream rushed in and after a moment of chaos, both brothers lay dead on the cold ground," Thrush concluded.

Maireen stopped and stared at Thrush, her eyes wide and wet, twinkling in the moonlight. "How horrible for that poor creature," she said.

Thrush stopped and turned around. A small smile grew on his face. "You know, that's the first time I've heard that response after telling that tale.

"The two brothers' fate, tragic, yes. But it was written for them. If it wasn't the púca, it would have been something else. And that creature did not hold the knife. But to think that your very existence could cause such grief, well, that's a true tragedy," she said as she took a step forward. She stared at Thrush.

"That's probably why this village still holds the most true to the traditions, at least when festivals are concerned. There was a lot of lost trust after that event. However, that was a long time ago, and time has a way of moving diluting such ways. It's not a bad thing, just the nature of the world," Thrush said.

Maireen's hand reached up towards Thrush's face. Through the periphery of her vision, she saw blue lights again rise from the bog. The air became electrified, she was certain this was no effect from exertion. Her fingers touched the side of Thrush's face and brushed away his dark hair. She explored the cheek scar with her fingertips. She opened her mouth to say something, but went silent as Thrush smiled and held her hand in his.

"*MAIREEN.*"

The horrible voice cut through the night and chilled her to her core. Before she could turn around, Thrush stepped forward and placed himself in front of her. She leaned her head past his body and saw in the distance the dark shadow of a horse with a dark rider. The moonlight made silhouette of the figure that bore no head on its shoulders, holding what looked to be a rigid whip at his side.

Thrush turned around and looked directly into her shimmering eyes, not widening with fear. "It looks like I was wrong about the identity of your pursuer, and for that, I apologize. But I promise you this, you will always have safe passage in these lands after tonight. Not man nor Aos sí will hinder your path. Now, Maireen, I'm going to ask you to turn around. The village is not too far and you will make it safely. But there is a price, you can't turn around. Just keep your eyes on that fire and walk straight to it. And when you arrive, you absolutely have to enjoy the festivities and not give another thought to him. Your name will never pass his lips after tonight," Thrush said and then kissed her forehead softly.

Maireen stood there, frozen as she watched Thrush's appearance change. First with long ears appearing on the sides of his head, much like an overgrown rabbit's. But no matter what changes took place, she just stared into his kind and deep eyes.

"Now, turn and go straight towards the bonfire. Don't stop until you've reached the clearing in the grove and its light warms you," Thrush said with a certainty in his tone.

Maireen blinked, tears rolled down her cheeks. She nodded and turned towards the bonfire. She drew a deep breath and called on her bravery, which was surprisingly easy this time. She realized that she fully trusted Thrush's words without falter. Her feet moved over the oak boards, the fire getting closer with every step. She heard Thrush yell, "I believe I need to have words with you." For a moment she was tempted to turn to his voice, but kept walking, her eyes straight without deviation. Even the floating wisps that surrounded her, clearly now, were no distraction. When she came to the edge of the bog and into the forest perimeter before the grove, she felt her facial muscles reach to a small but content smile. She continued on until the warmth of the fire wrapped around her like a woolen blanket. Only then did she turn around and look over the bog to see nothing but the moonlight reflect over the water.

Just as she found herself lost in the warmth of the fire, cheers and shouts erupted around her. She looked around to see the village folk surrounding her. Among the faces was Colm, a thin man of middle age who had been in her traveling party.

"Thank the heavens you're alright. You gave us such a fright. The entire village has been so worried. I've just arrived from a search endeavor myself," Colm said with a bright smile. He turned towards the crowd. "Send word, the girl is safe. Bring in all search parties! Make sure her uncle knows she has arrived safe."

A woman of grey hair and many lines earned by the years pushed her way past Colm and looked Maireen over as if she was inspecting an apple plucked from a tree. Her eyes worked up and down the young woman before settling on her lower leg. "Give her room you dolts, she's hurt. Bring her over to the feasting table, and bring some rags, and the poultice from my kitchen. The one in the green earthenware. The one above, oh nevermind, just bring them all," she commanded. At first the crowd stood, staring blankly at her commands until the woman raised a hand and brought it down on a young man's head. "The lot of you, fetch what I say," she demanded. The crowd scattered, most unaware of exactly where to go. The old woman brough Maileen to a bench at the table and examined her leg.

"It's fine, just a scratch," she protested as politely as she knew how.

"Even a scratch can be deadly," the woman said with a deepness of authority in her voice. She removed Maireen's makeshift bandage. "It's a deep cut, but you'll be fine once we treat it," Soon a young boy ran up to her with his arms filled with stone jars of various colors. She examined them and pulled a green jar from the precarious pile. She then proceeded to dip her fingers in the jar and salve the wound thick. "To think, we've been searching the forest high and low, and here you come traipsing out of the bogs as if you were one of the Aos sí, themselves. On a night like tonight, I would never have expected to see such a thing. I know you may not believe it, but there are things that live out there," she said as she patted Maireen's leg.

Marieen just smiled at the woman and nodded.

The thought passed her mind to tell of what happened to her since her separation earlier that evening. However, it was quickly diminished by Thrush's voice in her head, and the story he told her. She was content to keep that moment selfishly to just herself. The rest of the night was filled with feasting, drinking, tales told by her uncle of a distant childhood, and dancing, what little dancing the old woman allowed, citing the need for her leg to heal. She later found herself staring into the bonfire, then out into the bogs, warm with the thought that she would always be allowed safe passage on Samhain or any night.

On a hill some way off, two figures stood and overlooked the various bonfires from the remote villages below. The big figure was a headless man on top of a dark horse. A growling noise came from the hollow of his neck.

"I get it, you're mad. I took away your sport, but I just couldn't let you strike that woman down. She's too rare for such a fate," replied the creature, a mixture of man and beast, who stood with his arms folded over his chest.

The headless figure growled again.

"Fine, it's not sport, it's your duty. But look at it this way, who made those rules to begin with? Well, I'll tell you. It was them," he said while motioning to the villages below. "I remember a time before you took up the horse and, what is that, a whip made of a human spine? They've always had a talent for putting fire to their fears," he remarked. "What I'm saying is that you used to be without much form, an abstract. Well, they gave you form. Wait around a few hundred years, maybe a thousand, and you'll be something else. Maybe a feeble old man wandering town and road at night, for all I know. That's the fate for all of us really, to some extent."

Thrush smiled to himself. "We've been around long enough to know that while things change, there will always be stories people tell. Even when the steeple eclipses this night and her people entirely, those stories will keep. And I have no doubt this night will re-emerge and survive in some fashion, in ways we can only guess," he said as he turned and patted the horse's rear with his furred hands. "Perhaps a conversation for another time, old friend," he said as he walked into the night. The sound of his footsteps were replaced with the soft sound of a very swift rabbit running deep into the forest.

ABOUT THE AUTHORS

Jess Boldt is the writer of the novel *Disonia*, as well as several other works. He lives somewhere in the Midwest with his all-to-patient wife and brilliant daughter. He is currently working on a site for short stories, Tesoutroad.com

Andy Lockwood is a writer, artist, dreamer, and horror enthusiast. He is the author of three novels: *Empty Hallways, House of Thirteen,* and *Threshold*; a 12-part serial, *At Calendar's End,* and is a regular contributor to horror anthologies.

He lives in Michigan with his amazingly talented and entirely-too-supportive wife, a brood of cats, and a delightfully precocious goblin of a daughter. More information on his work is neglectfully curated at his website: www.happierthoughts.com

Jenifer Lynn is a writer, photographer, and video-game-enjoyer. She lives somewhere in the Midwest with a husband who tests her patience. She has two offspring whose brilliance she plans on living off of when she retires. She is currently working on the *Series of Echoes* books, and a collaboration fantasy novel with her aforementioned husband. You may find some of her work at www.tesoutroad.com.